The Rake
and the Muse

CHRISTINA DIANE

The Rake and the Muse

Unlikely Betrothal Series

Book Two

Copyright 2024 by Christina Diane

Edited by Emily Lawrence at Lawrence Editing

Cover Design by Erin at EDH Professionals

eBook ISBN: 978-1-964713-03-8

Paperback ISBN: 978-1-964713-11-3

Contents

Dedicated to those who are unwilling to give up the things they are most passionate about.

Note to Readers

I am so delighted and honored that you have picked up my book! Before you dive in, I would like you to know that I write for the modern reader. My stories are character-driven, fast-paced, and spicy with fun dialogue. While I love the Regency era and exploring the social constructs for the time period, I don't focus on complete historical accuracy. I complete research and attempt to create the setting and behaviors that are close to what you would expect of the era, but sometimes the characters and story have minds of their own. I wouldn't want you to be disappointed if you want a setting, themes, and language that are entirely accurate. If that is really important to you, this book might not be for you. And I understand!

Historical stories are a form of escape and are a fantasy in their own right, and I aim to help bring you to a world that might look and feel very much like the Regency era with diverse, inclusive characters who are fun, sexy, and intriguing as they find their path to love.

If you are excited about hard-headed and swoonworthy gentlemen, spirited and passionate heroines, fun banter, high spice, and guaranteed happily ever afters, set in my interpretation of the Regency era, then I hope you will keep reading and escape into a world of passion, romance, and sharp tongues.

Content Warnings

While this particular series isn't heavy on content warnings (but high on spice), I do my best to capture things I think a concerned reader might wish to know. If you ever feel I missed something, please message me on socials or christinadiane@christinadianebooks.com and I will update this list to improve the reading experience for other readers. To prevent spoilers, you can find content warnings for all of my published books here: https://christinadianebooks.com/content-warnings/

Chapter 1

LONDON, ENGLAND - SPRING 1813

J uliet Lane, the only child of the Earl of Avon, hid in the retiring room at the Fletchers' ball, doing her best to catch her breath after she practically sprinted down the hall. The retiring room seemed like the only place she might avoid getting asked to dance by any other gentleman with wandering hands. After what she had experienced on the dance floor with Lord Dunblane, she didn't much feel like dancing for the rest of the evening if she could help it.

Rejecting a dance with a gentleman just wasn't done, which left her vulnerable to such partners if she remained in the ballroom. Lord Dunblane took it upon himself to grasp her bottom during each of the turns so that no one might notice. When his hands weren't glued to her arse, his eyes were trained on her bosom. Which was hard to cover with the style of her dress and the way her stays positioned her ample breasts and made them appear even larger, if that were possible. She regretted that she hadn't worn a fichu and wouldn't ever make the same mistake again.

She was used to men staring at her, undressing her with their eyes. It was a usual occurrence at ton events. Juliet didn't possess the small body of the other misses on the Marriage Mart. They salivated and hardly noticed her face, let alone anything she might have to say, once they took notice of her body. Her figure was shaped more like an hourglass, with an abundant pair of full breasts and curvy hips, with a shapely arse.

The sound of voices reached her as someone approached the room, and she resolved to remain in her hiding place behind the screen.

"She probably went home," one young lady said. Juliet didn't recognize her voice and didn't dare peek her head out to see who it was.

"It makes you wonder," another lady started, "how the modiste has enough fabric to fashion a dress for those hips."

Both of the ladies laughed, proud of themselves. It wasn't anything Juliet hadn't heard before and she could only assume they were speaking about her.

In truth, the modiste had a terrible time fashioning dresses that were in high fashion because of her shape—not because of lack of fabric, but due to the current fashions, Juliet thought to herself. It was deuced annoying.

"Well, the gentlemen seem taken with her. It makes me wonder if we should start stuffing tissue paper into our stays."

"They shall never marry her. Wishing to dally with a woman and marrying her are quite different."

The ladies laughed again.

Juliet sensed another person had exited the screened area beside hers. "Lady Theodosia," another unique voice started. "There is nary a man alive who would wish to do either with you."

"You are one to talk," the one Juliet assumed to be Lady Theodosia said. "And where exactly is your husband, Lady Eliza?"

"Hopefully he doesn't exist," the voice sounding again like Lady Eliza replied. "Although, based on the three marriage offers I declined last week, perhaps I'll see if one of those heartbroken gentlemen might be desperate enough to saddle themselves to you."

Juliet covered her mouth to fight her laughter behind the screen. She didn't enjoy mocking others, but the lady certainly deserved a set down.

"Come, Rebecca," Lady Theodosia said. "We don't need to be seen with such company."

Once Juliet was certain the ladies had left, she emerged from her hiding place and the woman she believed could only be Lady Eliza was still in the room.

"Thank you for that," Juliet said, offering a small smile to the woman.

Lady Eliza shifted her attention to her and appeared surprised to find her standing there. Her expression shifted to a kind smile. "I can't stand those two," Lady Eliza replied. "Don't worry about them. They just envy the attention you get."

"I don't even want it," Juliet said, deciding to forgo the usual social protocol of feigning indifference and speak honestly with the lady who'd just come to her rescue. "I'm Lady Juliet, by the way."

"So glad to meet you. I'm Lady Eliza," the woman replied. "But please, just call me Eliza."

Juliet nodded in agreement.

"I don't much care for the attention either," Eliza shared. "I am uncertain if I ever wish to wed."

Juliet noted a pain in the woman's expression and assumed there was a reason for Eliza to make such a declaration, when she was almost certain it was the lady's first season out. Although, it was also Juliet's first season, and she shared a similar position on marriage.

"Would you like to come to tea at my house tomorrow?" Juliet asked, staring down at her feet. "I don't have many friends, and it would be nice to talk to someone who isn't as haughty as some of these other debutantes."

Eliza looped her arm in Juliet's. "I'd be delighted."

"Who did you say was joining for tea today?" Juliet's father, Earl of Avon, asked.

"Lady Eliza," Juliet replied. "The Earl of Nelson's daughter."

Her father nodded his approval. "I am glad to see you making friends, princess. You should find the season much more enjoyable without only your aunt to keep you company."

The previous evening had already been much more fun with Eliza at her side. They avoided most of the gentlemen, and they talked and laughed the evening away. The pair had become fast friends, and Juliet couldn't wait to learn more about her new friend and to entertain a guest for tea.

"I agree, Papa. You needn't join us, though. I'm sure we would just bore you with all the lady-like talk."

He laughed and patted her shoulder. "I shall make myself scarce. I hope you have an enjoyable time." Her father kissed the top of her head and then started for his study.

Juliet adored her father. Since her mother had passed when she was a young girl, he was all she had. She just didn't prefer him to linger around and listen to her conversations, especially the first time she'd have a friend come to call.

"My lady," her butler said, "you have a caller. Lady Eliza is here to see you."

"Thank you, White," she replied. "Please show her in here and bring tea."

He bowed and in a matter of moments, returned with Eliza.

"Juliet," she said, coming right to her and bussing her cheeks. "I am so glad to see you."

"Please, take a seat. Tea will be in shortly."

Eliza took the seat in the chair right next to where Juliet sat on the settee.

When Eliza glanced up at the wall, Juliet followed her gaze to see the paintings that she fixed her gaze on. "Who painted those? They are quite beautiful."

Juliet grinned and glanced at the paintings, pride radiating from her. "I did."

"You painted those?" Eliza asked, impressed. "You are talented, indeed."

A maid entered and rolled in the tea cart, interrupting their conversation. Once the maid departed, Juliet prepared them each a cup of tea.

Once they had their refreshments, Eliza stared at the paintings again. "Could you paint me?"

"I am certain I could," Juliet said.

"Your paintings should be in a gallery," Eliza said, her tone serious.

Juliet huffed. "I tried that, and the gallery wasn't interested in art from a woman, especially one from beau monde."

"How dare they!" Eliza exclaimed. Juliet couldn't agree more. Just another reason she and Eliza got on so well.

"I hope to open my own gallery one day. A gallery that will accept all work, regardless of gender, race, or class."

Eliza clasped her hands at her chest. "I love that! I shall be happy to help with your endeavor if I can. But I'm afraid I have no artistic abilities besides singing and the pianoforte."

"Just having your support is enough," Juliet said, beaming at her friend. "It shall be difficult to find others who will support the gallery, but I am determined."

"I have no doubt you shall succeed, Juliet," Eliza said, taking a sip of her tea. "You never told me why you were hiding in the bathroom last night."

Juliet huffed. "There are gentlemen who can't seem to keep their hands off certain places on my body."

Eliza rolled her eyes. "Just like a man to do whatever he wishes, with no concern for anyone else."

Juliet agreed, of course, but assumed her friend had different reasons for believing so.

Juliet contemplated Eliza's reaction. "Why is it you don't wish to wed?"

"I fancied myself in love once, and that was a farce," Eliza replied. "I have no desire to go through that again."

"What happened, if you don't mind me asking?" Juliet took a sip of her tea, awaiting the answer.

Eliza drew a deep breath. "I shall tell you the full story soon. I promise. Let us speak of more pleasant things today."

"I ask because I am uncertain a husband will support my artistic ventures, but I am so dreadfully curious about other benefits a marriage brings." She had tried to get her maid to tell her of such things to no avail.

Eliza laughed and gave her a knowing look. "Oh, I believe I understand your meaning."

Juliet's face flushed. "I don't care for these entitled men who grope me in ballrooms, but it might be nice to experience such things with a gentleman of interest. Whatever those things may be. With Mama gone, I shan't ask Papa to explain it to me."

"If that is what you wish to know, I can explain such things," Eliza said, grinning at her friend behind her teacup. "And I can tell you how to please yourself with no need of a man."

Chapter 2

NORFOLK, ENGLAND - SEPTEMBER 1814

J uliet took full advantage of the afternoon light in her window to continue working on her most recent painting. A woman who was with child had inspired her, and she wanted to capture the essence of motherhood with her paints. Women were so often hidden away in confinement while they were increasing, and she believed such a piece would make a great addition to her gallery one day. The world deserved to see the power and beauty of a woman with child. Why should women be forced out of society simply for growing a new life as their body was designed to do?

She had to create most of the painting from her own memory since she didn't have a live model present at the house party where she was in attendance with Eliza. They had arrived at Viscount and Viscountess Ockham's house party a couple of days ago. With around thirty guests in attendance, it was easy for Juliet to go unnoticed so she could take a bit of time each day to paint. She hadn't even been introduced to everyone at the party yet.

It was to her good fortune that her papa let her attend the house party without her aunt, or the woman would surely keep her hostage downstairs speaking with the eligible gentlemen.

With her newfound freedom, Juliet had hurried back to her chamber right after a game of Pall Mall on the lawn with the other guests, so that she could get in some work on her painting before dinner. Her absence should go unnoticed while the other ladies were busy with correspondence and needlepoint. Eliza would know where to find her and understood her need to spend a bit of the day with her canvas and paints.

A few hours passed without Juliet realizing it, lost in her work, completing a light sketch on her canvas ahead of beginning to paint the piece. She wanted to get the dimensions just right for how she wished to portray the woman in the image. She wasn't as confident in her sketching abilities, but painting was where she made the piece come alive.

"My lady," her maid said, pulling her focus from the canvas, "you shall be late for dinner if we don't dress soon."

"Of course, Bess," she replied. "I lost track of time."

Juliet enjoyed a glass of sherry in the salon after dinner. She had been surprised to find that Eliza was hiding in her room for the evening, avoiding the man who had broken her heart. She hated to see her strong, spirited friend in such turmoil and had suggested that Eliza consider taking a gentleman to her bed during the house party as a means to heal from what the man had put her through.

Scandalous for sure, but Juliet didn't see how it could hurt. Eliza would either get over the pain of her broken heart and push the man aside, or perhaps she would acknowledge that she still had feelings for him. She wasn't certain Eliza was ready to accept any notion of feelings for the man, even though it had been quite obvious to Juliet.

"Are you having a pleasant time so far, Juliet?" Rosina asked, approaching her.

"I am," she replied. "How about you?"

Rosina, Lady Preston, was one of the few who had always been kind to her. She had been married to Marquess Preston—a passionate love match from what Juliet had heard—for a brief time before he became very sick and passed away. It was awful that the woman had become a widow so young, not that she found herself without a gentleman in her company very often. Her reputation made her appear scandalous in the eyes of society, but Juliet had never worried about such associations. If Rosina wished to bed a man without marriage, then good for her.

The woman glanced around the room and Juliet noticed how she smiled in the direction of the Duke of St. Albans. "I believe I shall soon." She winked at Juliet as if they shared a secret.

Juliet laughed. "I wish I had the courage you do, my lady."

Rosina sighed and clasped one of Juliet's hands in hers. "It isn't courage," she replied. "I have just learnt to accept who I am and what I want. I don't let society decide what my future shall be."

Juliet wrenched her hands, fighting her nervous energy at the mere notion of considering such a thing for herself. "I'm trying."

"Don't try, my dear," Rosina said. "If you want something, make it yours."

"My ladies, you look lovely this evening," a gentleman's voice said, pulling Juliet's focus from their conversation.

"Lord Camden," Rosina said. "You look well."

Juliet glanced at the gentleman, and she couldn't help but notice how attractive he was. She had heard about him but hadn't actually been introduced. Given his rakish reputation, she hadn't hurried to make his acquaintance, assuming he would be much the same as the other men. His name occasionally appeared in scandal sheets for his rakish behavior, which would explain why he rarely appeared at balls and society events. A man of his reputation likely spent most of his time in brothels and gaming hells.

Such knowledge about his lifestyle didn't distract from the intensity of his masculine features and the effect they had on her.

"Indeed," Lord Camden replied, shifting his focus to Juliet. "And might I receive a proper introduction to this beautiful woman before me?"

Rosina snickered. "Camden, this is Lady Juliet," she introduced. "Juliet, this is Marquess Camden."

He took Juliet's hand and pressed his lips to it, which did something funny to her insides. His hair was a rich chestnut, which had a silky shine. When he looked up at her after kissing her hand, his eyes were a unique shade of light blue that bored into her with a wicked intensity.

The man was a rake, so there was no doubt he had the ability to render women senseless just from his presence. Masking the fortifying breath she drew, she fought to shake off the reaction to the far-too-handsome man.

"I am so glad to make your acquaintance, my lady," he said, his words smooth as butter.

"Pleased to meet you, my lord," Juliet replied.

He glanced at her chest, and she fought to roll her eyes. It was typical of every man she was introduced to, so she shouldn't expect anything different from a rake of the *ton*. To his credit, his eyes didn't linger, nor did he ogle her, so that was an improvement.

"I hope to see more of you while we are here, Lady Juliet," he said, bowing to her before continuing to another group of guests.

"So, you find him handsome, I take it," Rosina said, nudging her.

"No, of course not," Juliet returned. She noted Rosina's smirk and knew the woman didn't believe a word she said. "All right, he's very handsome," she admitted. Suddenly, something gnawed at her, even though she wasn't sure why she cared. "Is he one of your partners?" Juliet asked, unsure where she found the nerve to ask such a forward question.

Rosina laughed and patted her arm. "No. He has never warmed my bed," she said, assessing Lord Camden where he stood with his back to them across the room. "But I believe you should entertain such an arrangement."

"What?" Juliet scoffed, nervously glancing around the room. She knew her neck and face must be a deep pink. "I couldn't."

"You could, my dear. Just think about it."

Rosina was mad. Even if she knew the first thing about how to initiate such an entanglement with a man, she wasn't certain if she wished to do so. And even if he agreed to such a scandalous suggestion, it would be to use her once and never speak to her again. She wasn't certain why that bothered her, since that was what a tryst was meant to be. A moment of passion without the attachment. Juliet tamped down the notion, rejecting the idea. He wasn't for her, even if he was the most handsome man she had ever seen, from the front—and the back. His form was trim and muscular, but he had a rounded bottom that she could just barely make out beneath his tails when he turned to the side.

The room suddenly felt a bit warm, and she wished she had a fan so she might cool herself. The urge to touch such a gorgeous man heated her in the most inconvenient places while surrounded by all the other guests. Good thing she was aware of how to relieve the growing tension for herself.

Chapter 3

Theodore Pratt, the Marquess of Camden, or Theo as most of his friends called him, had found himself at a house party full of either eager marriage-minded chits or married couples. Neither would make for pleasurable company for a fortnight. He may be a rake, but dallying with innocents or married women typically led to far more drama and scandal than he wished to be embroiled in. There was the widow Lady Preston, but it was only a matter of time before she lost her heart again given how strong the love match between her and her husband had been.

It was far easier to take his pleasure from the women of the night, where they didn't ask questions. For a few extra coins, they also let him draw them. And as much as he loved fucking a beautiful woman, he might love drawing her just as much. Well, perhaps not quite as much, but close.

If he could dispense of the title and could pick anything he wished to do with his future, it would be to draw. To focus on his art and live the carefree life of an artist. That has been exactly what he planned to do until his older brother died and everything changed. Thomas had taken ill from pneumonia two years ago at the age of six-and-twenty and didn't survive the illness. Theo had been close to his older brother, even though they were three years apart in age. He mourned his brother's death for years and struggled daily with Thomas' voice in his head and how he missed him.

In some of his last moments with Thomas, his brother asked him to make a promise he never wished to make.

"Promise me, little brother," Thomas had said. "Promise me you will take care of our tenants. I know it isn't the life you want, but I need you to do what I shall be unable to do."

"I'll never fill your shoes. You will get better, and you shall continue to be the perfect marquess," he had replied, holding his brother's hand and fighting the ache in his heart.

Thomas had gripped his hand, using some of the last strength he had left in his then sickly body. He had once been a strong, broad-shouldered man. It had pained Theo to witness Thomas' decline.

"Protect our title, brother. We have always been a powerful, noble family. It's up to you to carry on our legacy." Thomas coughed a few times. "I need you to promise me."

"I promise, brother," Theo had said, his heart crushed at the impending loss of his dear brother.

Thomas was the one who had been born to be a marquess, not just in birth order, but for his sense of duty. Theo had never wanted any of it. Theo was the mischievous, wild child, living a devil-may-care life, even in his youth. His brother should have been the one to bring honor to the title. Theo could never be the man his brother had been.

But Thomas left him, and since he had never married, Theo was the marquess. He had a daunting set of responsibilities and expectations to live up to. In the eyes of society, he was expected to marry, sire an heir, and ensure the estates prospered. That would leave little room for him to pursue his true passion.

And his responsibilities held little appeal to him. Taking a wife would limit his ability to continue to practice his art, especially the type of drawings he completed as of late. Besides, he needn't be in a rush to take a wife. There would be someone willing to wed a marquess when he was ready to accept his fate. He'd be content to let the title go to some distant relative if he hadn't promised Thomas.

He did his best to do what he believed his brother would have wanted. He ensured the estates fared well, and he kept the title free from scandal. Sure, he was known as a rake, but as a man with a title, that hardly cast him out of society. Then, as often as he could in secret, he honed his artistry.

As much practice as he had, he still hadn't gotten it quite right on the page. There was always something off about the finished drawing. It left him with the same level of dissatisfaction as if he were worked up and ready to spend his cock but unable to do so. It was beyond irritating, indeed. At least he didn't possess the same issue when it came to actually spending his cock. A man could only take so much.

He continued to move on to the next woman, drawing her form—among doing other things—and hoping he might finally achieve what he had been looking for with his art and what he longed to capture on paper. He would know it when he saw it.

Theo glanced back at the lovely, tempting Lady Juliet. She didn't give him a second glance, which was abnormal for the simpering misses of the ton. There was some-thing different about her, something he couldn't quite pinpoint, and he found it intriguing. If he were honest with himself, everything about her was enticing. It wasn't just her beauty, which any man with eyes could easily identify. There was something about her presence that drew him in.

She was voluptuous in all the most perfect places, and he'd never been with a woman shaped like her. Her breasts were far more than ample, and he imagined her bottom was like a perfect, ripe, juicy peach, just waiting to be bitten into. More importantly, he longed to draw her above all else. Well, perhaps not above *all* else, but it was high on the list.

Not that such a thing would be possible. She was an unmarried young lady of his society, and it would be far too scandalous to strip her clothes from her. But her beautiful face and her luscious body were that of a siren, calling out to him and luring him in with its song. Theo imagined that her chocolate-colored hair, with strands that almost shined gold, would fall down her back in delicate waves that reached just above her lush bottom.

He had managed to get an introduction, then chastised himself for doing so. Theo was playing with fire, and his body would continue to be as unsatisfied as he had been with each of his finished drawings. He released a low growl behind his snifter of brandy. It was going to be a very long fortnight.

The next morning, he entered the breakfast room. He didn't take note of who all was seated and went straight for the sideboard. Theo made his selections, loading his plate. He'd always had a healthy appetite, especially at breakfast. A good day began with a good meal. He turned to take a seat and noticed Lady Juliet sitting at the table with an open seat to her right.

Unable to resist the opportunity to be in her presence and gaze upon her, and ever a glutton for punishment in the form of pain between his legs from unsated desire, he set his plate in front of the open seat.

"Might I join you, my lady?" he asked, pulling the chair out so he could sit.

She looked up at him, and something stirred in his ungentlemanly places—or very gentlemanly, depending on how one might look upon it. She was even more beautiful beneath the light of day than the lowly lit salon from the previous evening. And he had been practically ready to play the fool throwing pebbles at her window last night.

When he caught her gaze, he decided that he'd be content to fall into and swim in her grey eyes, which in the morning light took on an almost light purple color. He would sweep their plates to the floor and lay her across the table to feast on her if he weren't in better control of himself. She was alluring, to say the least, and he had to take his seat before she saw the telling ridge growing in his breeches.

"Of course, my lord."

Her voice was melodic and further threatened his good sense. He nodded to her and took a seat. Taking a bite of his eggs, he willed his desire to subside.

"I planned to ride this morning, my lord. Are you going to come?" she asked.

He choked on his bite of egg and took a drink of the glass of water in front of him on the table, pushing aside thoughts of what a ride from her might be like. "What was that?" he asked once he recovered, losing all wits to understand what she meant to ask about him. He didn't dare to hope she had asked about straddling him.

"There is a riding party departing after breakfast," she replied, eyeing him curiously. "I was just asking if you were going to join."

He drew a deep breath, clearing his mind of the nefarious thoughts that had crossed his mind at her previous words. "I believe I shall," he replied before he could think of the consequences of doing so. "Do you think you might wish to accompany me on the ride?"

What was he doing? She was erasing all of his good sense. Putting himself in her presence would not help the tension he now carried in his neck and shoulders. Horseback riding with a steel rod between his legs would be uncomfortable, to say the least.

"I would, my lord," she replied.

"Do you ride often, my lady?" he asked. His cock throbbed from the question. It was almost as if his dim-witted brain was torturing him on purpose, not allowing him to relent on imagining her in all manner of salacious positions.

She smiled at him, and his powerful reaction to such a simple expression bothered him far more than the notion of her taking a ride on his cock. He wouldn't allow himself to ponder that for a moment.

"I do. There is nothing quite like the wind blowing in one's hair and galloping across a field."

"I quite agree." He took a bite of his toast, doing his best to avoid the visual of her long hair flowing in the wind.

"Other than perhaps painting," she said. "That is the one thing that keeps me from spending as much time outdoors."

"Oh, so you paint?" he asked, genuinely curious to learn more about the subjects of her art.

"Juliet," Lady Eliza said from beside her. "We must change if we are to go on the ride."

Juliet nodded. "You are right," she said to her friend before returning her attention to Theo. "I shall see you shortly, my lord."

The ladies took their leave, and he sat at the table with a few other gentlemen. He kept his attention trained on his plate, not wishing to speak with any of them. His thoughts were consumed with the woman who became more intriguing to him by the minute, and he wasn't certain he cared to acknowledge it. No, he was certain. He didn't care to acknowledge it.

A half an hour later, Theo stood beside a large grey stallion that had just been saddled by a groom. Juliet stood nearby, holding the reins of a brown gelding. He watched as she used the mounting block and climbed atop the horse to sit side saddle atop the beast. Her movements were some of the most graceful he had ever seen.

She had a fluid way in which she moved, and he found he couldn't look away from her.

What in the devil was wrong with him? He wasn't the type of man who pined after a woman. He drew their form on parchment, he fucked them—sometimes twice—and he moved on to the next one. But his siren—no, not his—drove him to distraction, and he hadn't even had a taste of her sweet flesh. And as much as it pained him, he never would. She was a virgin, an innocent, and the most forbidden fruit if he wished to avoid scandal or marriage. Even if this particular fruit could be compared only to ambrosia.

Theo mounted his own horse, hoping that being in the saddle would give him something else to focus on. No such luck when she directed her horse to come up beside him, and he took notice of the way her chest moved as she trotted. He was a cad, looking at her as such, but he mentally defended himself in that he was equally drawn to everything about her, not just the large globes floating beneath her riding habit.

"It's a beautiful day, is it not?" she said, joy radiating from her. Her energy drew him in, and if he weren't more careful, he'd hang on her every word like one of the simpering misses he was so skilled at avoiding.

"It is," he replied. "Looks as if it might rain later, but we should have a pleasant ride."

The group departed and their horses fell in step together.

"So you mentioned you paint," he said, still curious about her art. "What kinds of subjects do you typically use to create your masterpieces?"

"I don't know if I would call them masterpieces, but anything really. I started with landscapes and inanimate objects and am focused on painting scenes with people now."

"Have you always painted?" He was curious if it might have been the same for her as it was for him. He hadn't personally known many others dedicated to art.

"As long as I can remember. I am at my happiest when I have a brush in my hand. I love to paint people and the world the way I see and feel it, not just recreate what it is in front of me."

His heart almost stopped beating at the way her eyes sparkled when she discussed her passions.

She shook her head, her cheeks adorably pinkened. "I'm probably not making any sense," she said.

He shook his head. "No, you are making complete sense," he replied. She understood, which was rare to find. "I feel the very same."

"Do you also paint, my lord?"

"I draw. Sketches. I bring my sketchbook with me almost everywhere I go." He gestured to his horse. "Perhaps not while horseback riding."

"I would love to see some of your work," she said.

He grinned. "Perhaps. But I shall need to see your work first to know if I would be too embarrassed by my lack of talent to match your own." He couldn't show her his drawings. Showing her drawing after drawing of the naked female form wouldn't be acceptable in the least. Neither was imagining her experiencing her first climax, and several more after that, on his cock, but that was beside the point.

"I am working on a piece here, actually," she replied. She glanced to see if anyone was listening to them before speaking again. "I shall sneak you into my chamber to see it if you wish."

He swallowed hard, not certain that it was the best idea to find himself alone in a bedchamber with her, but he was quickly losing control over himself to make sound decisions. Something else within him had taken over his responses. "I would very much like to see your painting." And so much more.

After riding for at least an hour, they reached where a picnic had been set up near the water. He remained enamored with her the entire time. They selected one of the blankets with a basket, and no one had joined them.

She told him all about some of her paintings, what paints she preferred, and the best lighting for her to do her work.

He shared how he had been fascinated with drawing since he could first hold a charcoal and some of his techniques. He described some drawings he had completed as a boy since those weren't scandalous to discuss in her presence.

Conversation came easily, and the time passed in an instant. He wasn't certain he had ever had such a lengthy conversation with a woman, nor revealed so much about himself to anyone besides Thomas.

When the entire group had finished their picnic, Theo went to stand. He brushed off his breeches and turned to help Juliet. He found Viscount Duncan already clasping her hands. He wasn't even certain where the man had come from.

"My lady, allow me," the man said. Theo looked at her delicate hands clasped around the man's and found he didn't care for it at all.

"Thank you, my lord," she said, smiling up at the man.

Duncan put her hand in the crook of his arm and escorted her away from the picnic area back towards the horses. Theo followed behind them, listening as best as he could.

"Are you having a pleasant afternoon, my lady?"

"I am, my lord. Are you?"

"It is not as enjoyable as partnering with you in Pall Mall yesterday, but it appears to be looking up."

"Indeed," she said, glancing back towards Theo.

Duncan glanced over his shoulder and smirked at Theo, then returned his attention to Juliet. "I hope to get to know you better over the next several days," Duncan said, looking down at Juliet's chest, but Theo was almost certain she hadn't noticed. He had the urge to shove the man into the grass and refused to think about where such a notion came from.

"I would enjoy that, my lord," she said. Theo noticed she didn't sound overly eager about the notion, so perhaps she was merely being polite.

She glanced back at Theo as if she were looking for him. Unfortunately, Duncan took note.

"My friend, Camden, here, has no intention of marrying," Duncan said, "while I am hoping to find a great love."

Theo wanted to punch the sweet smile off the man's face. He would appear churlish if he mentioned he wasn't friends with the man, but Duncan wasn't wrong that Theo didn't have any intention of marrying. Not for a very long time, if ever. Although, based on some of the man's evening companions, Theo wasn't certain he believed a love match was the reason for Duncan's interest in Juliet.

Juliet glanced at Theo, and he fought to keep the scowl from forming on his face.

"Unless you have changed your mind about marriage, Camden?" he asked. The bounder knew what he was doing, attempting to make himself more appealing to Juliet, while reminding her that Theo was nothing but a rake. And Theo couldn't even argue that point, although he hadn't ever taken an innocent to his bed. He had some honor, even if it were hanging on by a very loose thread the more time he spent in Juliet's presence.

"I can't say that I have, Duncan," Theo said, grounding out the words with a tight smile.

Duncan laughed. "Best to look out for this one, my lady."

She glanced at Theo and offered him a small smile.

"Lord Camden has been nothing but a gentleman in my presence," she said, giving Theo a kind nod.

"I am glad to hear it, my lady," the man said. "Here, allow me to assist you with your horse."

He placed his hands on her hips and helped to lift her into her sidesaddle. Theo groaned to himself, mostly for the man's hands being on her, and to tamp down his own desire to feel her lush form.

"Thank you, my lord."

Theo hopped into his saddle and walked his horse next to hers to ensure he would be beside her for the ride back.

But the odious Duncan caught up to them, joining her on the other side. The man kept her focus on him, asking her about her country home and how her father fared. Theo couldn't get a word in, but he also didn't wish to discuss the things he had shared with her in the presence of another, especially Duncan.

Juliet's horse began to slow its pace. "I believe my horse will struggle to keep up, as I must slow down."

Theo took his opportunity. "Duncan, will you ride ahead and alert the stables that we may need another horse? I shall stay with the lady in the event she needs assistance."

As if they had planned it, Juliet smiled at the man. "I would be most appreciative of your assistance, my lord."

Theo couldn't help himself and smirked at the man where Juliet couldn't see. The man smiled, but it didn't reach his eyes. "It is no trouble, my lady. I am happy to be your white knight."

Duncan rode off, and Theo was left alone with Juliet. The rest of the party created further distance between them, given the slow pace that Theo and Juliet now traveled.

Theo noted the dark clouds in the sky and hoped they would make it back before the rain began and soaked them.

He wasn't certain if Juliet might have an interest in Duncan and decided to take the high road and not speak poorly of the man. Even though he wished to rearrange the chap's face.

"It is surprising that your father allowed you to attend a house party on your own," Theo finally said.

She shrugged. "Papa knew Eliza would be with me, and he thinks highly of our hosts," she replied. "He made sure to give me a lecture before he left."

"What is it that fathers lecture their unwed daughters about?" He had an idea, and he was almost certain her father wouldn't appreciate Theo being anywhere within his daughter's presence.

"No sneaking off with a gentleman, avoid men who defile innocents, only accept a man who will love and respect me as I am," she said, waving her hand. "Things like that."

"So your father hopes for you to find a love match?" he asked. Such a thing was rare in their society. Theo wasn't certain he was even capable of the emotion any longer. Losing his brother hardened his heart to feel much for anyone or anything, other than the promise he made and his art—and a good tup. He wasn't fool enough to mistake passion for love.

She nodded. "Very much so. He was very much in love with my mama." She paused and glanced over at him. "In truth, I'm not certain I wish to wed."

"I'm not certain I have met a young lady who didn't have her heart set on marriage."

"I have my painting and my own dreams and plans. I couldn't marry a man who would interfere and not allow me to pursue my craft."

Theo could relate. He had similar feelings about his drawing. Society would frown on a titled peer publicly pursuing his art, but what he did away from the eye of the *ton* was of no consequence. He had promised his brother he would protect the title and estates, and being ostracized from society for being paid for his drawings would not uphold that promise. So he drew in private. Only Juliet was aware—to an extent—of his secret, if you could call it that. He imagined it was far worse for a woman set on pursuing such things.

Her horse suddenly stopped and slowed its pace, startled by another loud rumble of thunder. "I don't believe he can continue, my lord."

She climbed from her gelding, and Theo halted his horse and jumped down to join her.

"Please, call me Theo. I know it isn't proper, but I give you leave to do so when we are alone. The formalities feel wholly unnecessary after all we have shared with each other."

Juliet petted her horse. "All right, Theo," she said, trying it out. He found he quite liked the way she said his name. "But you must call me Juliet or Jules. Only my closest friends do so."

"Jules," he said, "It suits you."

There was another crack of lightning and then an enormous crash of thunder. Juliet jumped, and in a quick reaction, Theo pulled her into his arms. She smelled of jasmine, and he fought not to bury his nose into her neck and hair.

"I believe we are going to get drenched, Theo."

The sound of his nickname on her tongue only heightened his desire to keep holding her against him.

Forcing himself to release her, he stepped back and looked up at the sky. "We must tie up your horse and send someone to fetch him. You shall ride with me, and I will try to get us back as quickly as possible."

She looked up at him. "If you are certain."

"I don't want you to catch a cold from getting caught in the rain," he said.

He looked back at his horse and the realization that she would ride on his lap hit him and his cock twitched in response. She was going to tempt him to distraction. It was as if the universe was testing him and his ability to maintain his honor. But he meant what he said, and he had to get her back as quickly as possible.

A raindrop hit her cheek, and he instinctively brushed it away with his thumb. An action that was far too intimate, and he wasn't certain why he did so.

"I think you are right," she said, glancing up at the sky.

He tied the reins of her horse to a nearby tree, ensuring it was safely under the cover its leaves provided, then grabbed Juliet's hand, pulling her with him to his own horse.

"I will pull you up in just a moment. You are going to need to straddle me so we can return quickly."

She nodded and wrapped her arms around herself as the wind picked up.

He drew a steadying breath and hopped into his saddle. Once seated, he reached down for her and pulled her to him. She swung her leg over the horse and lifted her skirts so she could straddle his lap. Once she was seated, he was far too aware that her cunt was pressed against his cock. The dratted fabric from his breeches served as a barrier. He was already half erect before he had pulled her up, so he could only hope she wouldn't notice when the bulge grew harder.

She shivered, and he pulled her close. "Wrap your arms around me and hold on."

Juliet did as he said and her head rested on his shoulder, facing him, so his chin blocked some of the raindrops from her face. He glanced down at her, and his heart nearly leapt from his chest. She was the most beautiful woman he had ever seen.

"Are you ready?" he asked, his voice a gravelly whisper.

She nodded against him.

He flicked the reins and started his horse. Once he increased speed, he wrapped one of his arms around her to ensure she was secure against him. The scent of jasmine and the feel of her soft, voluptuous form against him drove him to distraction. With every canter, it bounced her on top of his lap, sending small waves of pleasure coursing through him. Part of him hoped she felt it, too. Part of him hoped the movement might give her a first taste of pleasure, even if an unorthodox one.

He was far too tempted to ditch the notion of returning to the stables and find one of the hunting cabins to take her to instead. Shaking off the urge and remembering his honor, he continued and resolved to return to the stables.

The rain picked up, and the droplets streamed down his face. She gripped him tighter and buried her face in his neck. He had some unspoken need to protect her. He tightened his hold on her and rested his chin on her head. The maddening rock of her hips on his being was just enough to make him acutely aware that a beautiful woman sat on his lap and stoked every flame of desire, but was not quite enough pressure to drive him to spend.

They caught up with the rest of the riding party just as everyone reached the stables.

Part of him was annoyed that he had to remove her from his hold, but he needed to get her warm and dry. He also needed to get his cock to settle, and that wouldn't be possible with her in his arms.

He lifted her down to her feet, hoping the others wouldn't notice how they rode in together. He hopped down and caught a groom's attention to let him know about the horse they had left behind. Duncan must have ditched his mission to provide any aid when the rain began. *Some knight*, Theo huffed to himself.

"Please allow me to escort you to your chamber to seek dry clothes. It's the least I can do, Jules." Where was his mind to overrule the wants of his body and his heart? No, not his heart. That would be utter madness.

Chapter 4

Juliet's breath caught, allowing her imagination to run wild at the mention of Theo escorting her upstairs to her chamber. "Thank you, Theo," she managed to say in response.

She had only hoped she hadn't left his breeches damp from how aroused she had been pressed against him. She knew enough to know that she was pressed against his cock, and based on the hardness of it, he wasn't without notice either. The realization only made her arousal even greater.

Where conversation had come so easily between them all day, she was at a loss for what to say as they ascended the grand staircase together. She was certain her skin was flushed all over from where it heated, and she pushed aside all of her wicked thoughts. He wasn't the man for her, even if he appreciated art. She wasn't even certain she wanted a man to begin with. It was only natural that in the situation they were put in, that there would be a bit of instinctual arousal from their bodies, right?

They reached her door, and she looked around to see if anyone was in the hallway. Before her good sense could stop her, she opened her door and pulled him in with her.

"This seemed like the most opportune time to show you my painting," she said when he looked at her with surprise. "We might not get the chance again without someone seeing us."

At least she told herself that was why she pulled him in. It certainly wasn't because she didn't wish to depart from him yet.

"Ah, quite right," he said, seeming to shift on his feet as if he were uncomfortable. "I would like to see it."

She pulled him to the easel next to the window and let him see the canvas where she had sketched out a few lines to serve as the foundation for the piece and where she had started painting the body of the woman. Her stomach was in knots as he assessed her work. She wasn't sure why, but she wanted him to appreciate and see the value in her art.

He looked at it thoughtfully, and every moment that went by where he didn't say something made her stomach tense tighter.

"You are quite talented," he finally said. "I mean it. I see where you are going with the piece, and I can't wait to see it finished. Please tell me you will allow me to do so."

She beamed at him. "Thank you, Theo. And of course you may."

"Did you have a model sit for you?"

She shook her head. "No, I was inspired when I saw a woman with a rounded belly and created the likeness the way I wanted it."

He turned to face her. "You are impressive, Jules."

"I would still love to see your work." She wanted more than anything to see what he drew. She was curious what would capture his attention and how he would translate it on paper.

"I don't know if mine could compete with yours," he said, glancing back at her painting. "You might take pity on me."

She touched his arm and forced herself to ignore the electricity she felt, even though she wasn't even touching his skin. "I have no doubt your work is extraordinary."

His gaze locked on hers and they stared at each other for a few moments, neither looking away. He took a step closer to her so there were only a few inches between them.

She thought he might lower his mouth to hers, and she shivered from anticipation. The movement captured his attention, and he appeared to shake off his thoughts.

"You must be freezing, Jules. I shall depart so that we might get out of these wet clothes. I shall see you at dinner."

She swallowed hard and nodded. She wasn't sure where her words had gone. Perhaps it was the mental image of him peeling away the wet clothes from what was an obviously muscled frame, if his broad shoulders and taut legs were any indication.

He strode to the door and opened it slowly to peek out and see if anyone was in the hallway. He glanced back at her and grinned before disappearing to the other side of her door.

Her entire body was heated from being in his presence that she wasn't certain the cold, wet clothing had any impact on her. Sighing, she reached for the bellpull so that Bess could help her get out of her wet riding habit.

A few minutes later, Bess appeared. She had a warm bath brought up. Once Juliet had bathed and soaked in the warm water, Bess helped her to dress in a dinner gown. Juliet sat at the vanity and let her maid brush her now-dry hair and style it into a simple chignon for dinner.

As soon as Bess finished, Juliet jumped up from her chair, wanting to work on an idea that came to her. She grabbed another piece of canvas and began sketching. Juliet worked on her sketch until she knew she would need to fetch Eliza to join for dinner. She hid her work behind the other canvas on the easel and departed to venture to the next door over where Eliza was staying.

Eliza had skipped out on dinner the previous night to avoid her past love, and Juliet wouldn't allow her to do the same that evening. Juliet's mind was muddled, and her body was still aflame. She needed the company of her best friend at dinner, if only to give her someone to talk to while she attempted to distract herself from her wicked thoughts.

When they entered the salon, Juliet was instantly aware of where Theo was. She didn't tell Eliza about her encounter with the man, or that she referred to him as Theo. Her friend would read far too much into it. Perhaps she would tell her tomorrow once she had sorted out her thoughts, or at least gave herself a release from her own hand so she might have her wits about her again.

Theo's eyes were on her, and he nodded at her when she caught his gaze. She wasn't sure if she was annoyed or relieved that he didn't come to greet her. It would have put her in an odd spot with Eliza, especially after she had given her friend such a hard time yesterday about not telling her that her past love, Nick, was in attendance at the party.

She smiled back at him and selected a glass of sherry for herself.

"I saw you riding with Lord Camden today," Eliza said. "Did you have an enjoyable time?"

"What? Oh, yes. He is a good conversationalist."

Eliza gave her a knowing look and leaned closer. "Perhaps you are the one who should consider a tryst?"

Juliet's face heated, and the room was far too warm for her liking. "Rosina said the same thing. You are both mad."

"I don't think I am."

"What about you?" Juliet asked, shifting the focus away from Theo. "Is Lord Irvine going to appear in your chamber tonight?"

Eliza huffed. "I don't know. Nick is everywhere I turn, and I don't know what I feel with him so near. I'm still thinking about it."

Juliet suspected her friend had much stronger feelings for Nick than she was ready to admit, but Eliza would have to work through it on her own.

Their hosts, Lord and Lady Ockham, began leading the party to reconvene in the dining room for dinner. Lord Irvine appeared to escort Eliza. Juliet followed, and an electric shock coursed through her body before she looked to her left and realized that Theo stood next to her, extending his arm.

"You looked in need of an escort, my lady."

She smirked at the return to formalities while surrounded by the other guests. "Haven't you been my hero enough times today?"

"What can I say? Perhaps saving beautiful young ladies is my new calling."

"If you need a reference, I'd be happy to give one," she replied, smiling up at him. She had never flirted with a gentleman before, and she found she quite enjoyed it. Perhaps too much. Or perhaps it was him that she enjoyed the most.

He seated her in her place in the dining room, then took his own seat, which was directly across from her. She would spend the entire meal with him directly in her line of sight.

Theo glanced across the table at her and appeared as if he were contemplating something. He didn't speak with anyone and seemed to work something out in his head. She forced herself to look away so he wouldn't think she was staring at him. Even if she was.

Lord Duncan was seated to her right, and he wasted no time starting up a conversation with her.

"I hope you are feeling well after getting caught in the rain, my lady."

"I am well. Thank you for the concern."

He smiled at her. "Glad to hear it," he said. "I believe there will be a trip to the village tomorrow. I hoped you might accompany me."

She glanced at Theo, who was looking down at his plate. Lord Duncan was handsome but not nearly as much so as Theo. There was something about Duncan that made her uneasy, even though he had technically done nothing that was untoward. Other than constantly stare at her chest, she reminded herself. She supposed he also tried to make Theo look bad in her eyes, which wasn't well done of him.

"Of course, my lord." It was polite to accept him, even though she wasn't certain she preferred him as her escort. "I hope you won't mind if Lady Eliza joins as well. She will wish to attend with me." She could have Eliza assess him as well and see what she thought about the man.

"Not at all. I would imagine Lord Irvine will join our small party from the looks of things."

Juliet glanced down at the other end of the table and saw the pair in conversation. "You may be right about that."

Dinner passed by with nothing of note. Polite conversation from those who were seated around her. She couldn't help but notice that Theo remained quiet unless someone spoke directly to him, and part of her wondered if something was amiss.

The ladies departed the dining room to leave the gentlemen to enjoy their port. They decided they would take turns playing the pianoforte and singing for the group once the gentlemen arrived. Juliet and Eliza would perform a duet they had played together a few times before.

Once the gentleman arrived, she watched the door for Theo to enter. When he did, she continued watching him as he grabbed a tumbler of brandy from the sideboard.

When the first woman took her turn at the pianoforte, she glanced at him again and noted that he stared at his glass, not paying attention. He did the same with the next performer.

Eliza grabbed her hand and pulled them both to take their seats on the bench. They didn't need sheet music since they had performed the song so many times, so they played and sang. Juliet's fingers were comfortable and familiar, moving across the keys. She glanced up and caught Theo staring at her. Her voice almost caught, but she recovered and kept singing. She glanced at him again, and his gaze remained fixed on her.

Her entire body thrummed. The place between her thighs was damp, and she clenched them together, attempting to ease her discomfort. She closed her eyes, singing and trying her best not to think about straddling him.

When the song was over, the room erupted into applause. Lord Irvine approached the bench and took Eliza's hand, leading her to the terrace.

An outstretched hand appeared to her right, and she knew without looking up that the hand belonged to Theo. "My lady."

She clasped his large hand, allowing him to help her stand and move away from the pianoforte. He shifted her hand to the crook of his arm.

"Is there anything you can't do?" he asked.

"Embroidery," she deadpanned. "I'm atrocious. I shan't ever stitch you a handkerchief."

"Noted," he replied. "I shall have to settle for the plain white ones."

Another performer positioned herself at the pianoforte and began playing. Juliet stood there, attempting to listen, but her attention was continually drawn to the feel of Theo's firm bicep beneath her fingers.

There were a few more performances. After the final one, all the guests began making their way to their chambers. She glanced up at Theo. He appeared to be lost in thought, as he had much of the evening.

She glanced around and there wasn't anyone in earshot. "Is something amiss, Theo?"

He appeared to shake off his thoughts. He opened and closed his mouth again before finally responding. "Not at all."

"It appears the evening has come to a close."

"I believe you are right, Jules," he replied, keeping his voice low. "I shall escort you upstairs."

They climbed the stairs together, and when they reached the top, she released his arm. It would be far too scandalous, with the rest of the houseguests moving about for him to escort her all the way to her chamber. Besides, he wasn't courting her. She wasn't sure what he was doing, precisely, but she found herself wondering what he looked like beneath his clothing. And such thoughts could be problematic.

"Good night, Theo," she said, looking up at him in the dark hallway, his chiseled face far more intense and heart-stoppingly handsome with only the low candle-light.

"Good night, Jules."

She released his arm and continued to her chamber. Bess was waiting for her when she arrived to help Juliet ready herself for bed. Juliet completed her evening ablutions and changed into her night rail. Bess brushed out her hair and fixed it into a long, loose plait. A fire had been tended in her chamber, so the room was warm and cozy as she prepared to climb into bed.

She released Bess for the evening and seated herself before the fire, staring at it. Theo unleashed something in her. Something wanton. She had done little but imagine what he would feel, look, and taste like if he were naked before her. What his kiss might be like. What that hard bulge she rubbed up against might feel like inside her.

The dampness pooled between her thighs again. Thankfully, within the privacy of her room, she could finally do something about it. Eliza had told her everything about what coupling with a man was like and how she could give herself a release from her own hand. The knowledge had been useful, and she was badly in need of such release.

She rose from the settee and crossed the room to climb into her bed. She lay back and replayed the memory of her thighs wrapped around Theo's torso. With each bounce of the horse, she rubbed against him.

Wanting to recreate the fantasy, she came up onto her knees. She spread her thighs open, simulating the position she was in when she straddled him. She pulled her night rail over her head, as the fabric was in her way, leaving her completely naked.

She cupped her left breast in her hand and ran her thumb back and forth across her nipple. Reaching her right hand between her legs, she found the sensitive place that had rubbed against his cock and circled it with her

finger. She let her head fall back and continued the movement with her fingers while she massaged her breast,
releasing a low moan.

Juliet was so entranced by her imaginings that she
missed the soft knock at her door.

"Jules?"

Chapter 5

I t had been on the tip of Theo's tongue all night to ask her if he could draw her. She was an artist, and she might not be so scandalized to allow him to do so. Perhaps if he could draw her, he might get her out of his head. He craved to explore every inch of her, but at least if she allowed him to capture her form on paper, he could look without touching.

He needed to discuss it with her in private, since the mere notion would ruin her and require them to wed. The house party created a unique opportunity where they could do so with no one the wiser if they were careful.

He paced his chamber, wearing nothing but his breeches and a button-down white shirt. Would she box him on his ears for even suggesting such a thing? He worked up his nerve and resolved to ask her and give her the choice. If nothing else, even if she said no, perhaps it would help put the notion behind him and give some ease to the unrelenting erection between his legs.

Theo grabbed his leather satchel, which held his drawings, and slowly opened his door, poking his head out to confirm if the hallway was empty. He saw Lord Craven head from the staircase towards the wing where Juliet's room was. He waited a few moments, giving the lord a chance to get where he was going. Then he crept along barefoot, remaining in the shadows until he reached her chamber.

He rapped his knuckles on the door and waited. The longer he remained outside her door in the hallway, the greater risk he had of being caught doing so. He quietly tried the knob and was relieved that it had turned. He'd need to alert her to his presence right away so she didn't scream and alert the entire house to his appearance in her chamber.

He closed the door behind him and locked it so no one could enter and find him there. He glanced over at the bed and his cock throbbed even harder at what he saw.

"Jules?" Her name came out low and gravelly on his tongue.

She jumped and pulled her hands away from where she pleasured herself. Her body was on full display before him, and he couldn't look away. Her breasts were full and large. Both of his hands might not fit around one of them. Her waist curved in, creating a perfect holding place to grasp her full hips. He only wished he could get a look at her naked arse as he imagined it was a thing of perfection. If he were a poet, he would write sonnets about her form.

"What are you doing here?" she asked, panic overtaking her tone. Grabbing the sheet from her bed to hold up in front of herself, she then sat back on her knees. Damn that sheet.

"I came to ask you something, but I have a whole slew of new questions," he said, taking a few steps closer to her bed, and sat the satchel in a chair.

She didn't meet his eyes and tried to cover her face with her hand. "Pardon me while I just die of embarrassment," she said, using her other hand to better position the sheet around her body.

He stepped up next to the bed and moved her hand away from her face. He imagined she would be the darkest shade of red if there were more light in the room. "Please. You have nothing to be embarrassed about. I like what I see very much. You are quite beautiful, Jules."

"I was just…"

"Pleasuring yourself?" he finished for her. Part of him regretted getting her attention because watching her do so might have been better than drawing.

She nodded.

"Where did you learn such things? And please don't tell me from another man." He didn't like the thought of that one bit.

"A friend told me," she responded, the shyness prevalent in her tone. "It comes in quite useful when one isn't certain about marrying."

"And was this friend a man?" he asked. His blood boiled from the mere notion of a man speaking the words to her.

She shook her head. "A female friend who was… experienced."

"Good." He released a long breath.

"Why is that good?"

He shifted himself to stand directly in front of her. "Because I'm not certain I wish to imagine that anyone else had seen you this way." He wasn't sure why he felt that way, or why he would admit it to her, but he would thrash any man who attempted to do so.

She swallowed hard.

"What were you thinking about?" he asked.

She shook her head.

He cupped her chin with his hand and leaned his face closer to her, nodding. "Tell me." He would get it out of her.

"I can't."

"Were you thinking about me?" He had a feeling she was based on her reaction to him, and his cock was the hardest it had ever been waiting for her response. His honor slowly evaporated the more their conversation continued.

She froze, then closed her eyes and nodded. "Yes."

He lowered his lips to her ear. "Good girl," he whispered. "Were you imagining what I might look like without clothing?"

She nodded, barely meeting his eye. He found her newfound shyness charming, given what he walked in on. She was a goddess who knew what it meant to take her pleasure, and he'd help her feel that way again in his presence.

He unbuttoned his shirt, taking each button slow and steady while he caught her gaze. Once he had unfastened all the buttons, he removed the shirt and tossed it aside. Then he unbuttoned his breeches and pushed them down to the floor. He knew he shouldn't, but he couldn't help himself. She had him under her spell.

He held his arms out so she could get a look at him in the candlelight. "Touch me anywhere you wish. As long as I get to touch you in all the same places." It only seemed fair, after all. He wondered if she might kick him out of her room for a few moments while she contemplated him.

But then she pushed herself back up higher onto her knees and took in his form. Even in the low lighting, he could see the desire and intrigue in her eyes. The realization made his shaft twitch. She didn't appear to notice as she reached out her hand and grazed her fingers across his hard chest with a smattering of hair.

"I feel like it's only fair that you drop your sheet, don't you think?" There wasn't a bit of rational gentlemanly sense left. He was all primal man standing before the most tempting of women.

She raised her chin and caught his gaze, then let the sheet fall to the bed. He saw the confidence returning to her and couldn't wait to see what she would do.

She brought her other hand to his chest so that both palms rubbed across him. Her hands were the softest he'd ever felt on his skin. It took every ounce of his remaining control to keep his arms at his sides and not shift her beneath him on her bed.

Juliet shifted one hand up his neck and into his hair, running her fingers through it.

"I had a feeling your hair would be silky to the touch," she said. So she had thought about touching him all over, too.

"Is that all you were curious about, Jules?" He wanted her hands all over his body, far more than she even realized.

She shifted her other hand down his trim waist to his hip. He held his breath, hoping she might take his cock in her hand, but she slipped her hand lower and massaged his thigh.

"You are so muscular," she said, almost with a sigh.

Her hand moved again, and this time she cupped the cheek of his arse. The anticipation was almost more than he could bear, waiting for her to touch him in the place where he throbbed for her.

As if she heard his plea, her fingers danced along his hip before running a single finger along the head of his cock, causing him to move against her hand.

Her fingers continued along his shaft, rubbing up and down his length.

"I didn't expect it to be so soft to the touch, given how much it sticks up."

"You can make a fist around it," he choked out.

She did as he said, and he groaned, moving himself so she stroked him with her hand.

"My turn," he ground out. She'd make him spend before he had a chance to touch her. He may not be acting as the proper gentleman, but he'd be damned if he took his pleasure from the lady before he ensured she was thoroughly sated.

Theo clasped her hips and traced his hands up the sides of her body until he reached the large flesh of her breasts.

He cupped one in each hand, massaging and lifting them. He ran his thumbs along her tightly budded nipples and flashed a wolfish grin when she gasped.

"These are perfect."

He released her breasts and ran his hands around her and slid them down until he could cup the flesh of her arse. He closed his eyes and fought the thoughts of what he would love to do if he turned her around.

"This is even better."

He left one hand clasping her bottom and shifted his right hand to her front. He reached between her legs and slipped one finger into her wet folds.

"You are so wet. And that just might be the best."

She moaned and spread her knees wider when he inserted his finger deep inside of her.

He withdrew and entered again.

"Have you ever tasted yourself?" He was being far too wicked, forgetting that she was an innocent. Although in his defense, he did walk in on her fingering herself while propped on her knees.

She shook her head.

Unable to stop himself, he removed his finger and brought it to her lips. She didn't hesitate to suck his finger all the way into her mouth, licking and sucking it clean. His cock throbbed and his eyes rolled back in his head from the intensity that she sucked his finger.

"What was I doing to you in this fantasy of yours?" He wouldn't take her virtue, even though his cock would hate him for it, but if she would allow him to make her come, he would certainly do that.

"I was on top of you, like when we were on the horse," she said, her words quick.

"Ah, so my hard cock teased you earlier?" He grinned, validating that she had been aroused from bouncing against his cock.

She nodded and captured his gaze.

"Your wet cunt teased me, too," he said. "I can make you come that way without taking your virginity."

Her eyelids were hooded and heavy, and she licked her lips.

"Would you like me to show you?" he asked.

"Please, Theo."

He sat beside her on the bed and helped her to straddle him, each of her knees planted on the bed against his thighs. His cock was hard and jutting up between them.

"Put two fingers inside yourself," he ground out.

She gripped his shoulder with one hand and used the other to reach between her legs and insert two fingers just as he had instructed, undulating against her hand. He fisted his cock and stroked it as he watched the siren pleasuring herself on top of him.

"Now rub the wetness from your fingers onto the sensitive place outside of your core." She shifted her hand up. "That's it. Circle your fingers there."

He bit into his bottom lip when she moaned and wet her nub. He wanted nothing more than to have her straddle his face and let him feast on her. He just might do so if she allowed him such an indulgence.

Needing a taste of her, he grabbed her hand and brought it to his lips, taking both of her fingers in his mouth to get what taste he could.

"You are better than the sweetest honey," he said. "Now move your hips like you are fucking me and rub yourself against my cock."

She scooted closer and rocked her hips against him. He let her set the pace and watched her in awe as her perfect, lush body moved against him. Unable to rest any longer, he clasped her bottom. He spread her cheeks and helped her to move.

"Theo," she moaned when he brought her tight against his hard shaft.

With her cheeks spread, he slipped two fingers inside of her heat from behind so she fucked his fingers while she teased her pearl with his cock.

His shaft throbbed from the way she moved against him, and he couldn't wait to watch her shatter on top of him.

With his fingers still inside of her and one hand helping to move her faster, her breath became wild and labored. Then her slick heat clenched around his fingers, and she undulated when she cried out, letting her head fall back.

Theo removed his fingers from inside her and fisted himself. He used her wetness from his fingers to increase the friction when he stroked himself, only needing a few more fast strokes before his cock erupted between them.

She lifted herself off him and shifted to sit beside him on the bed. He put his arm around her, and she leaned against him, resting her head on his shoulder.

"This isn't what I came here for," he said. "But I have no complaints."

She picked up her head and looked at him curiously. "Then why did you sneak into my room in the middle of the night?"

He cleared his throat. "I wanted to know if you would allow me to draw you."

"Draw me?"

He climbed off the bed and went to the washbasin. He dampened a clean cloth and brought it back to the bed.

"Allow me to clean you first." Although he quite liked seeing her waist coated in streaks of his seed.

She nodded, and he gently wiped between her legs and her stomach. He wiped himself clean and then set the rag on the table.

Theo picked up the leather satchel and opened it, retrieving pieces of parchment from inside. He handed them to her.

Juliet looked at the drawings. She held them closer to the candlelight so she could get a better look. He realized how nervous he was for her to see them. He had never shown anyone any of his drawings before, not even the subjects of the drawings.

"These are beautiful, Theo."

He appreciated her words and was relieved that she didn't laugh at him or pity his inferior skill.

"There is something off with them."

She looked at them again and assessed each one. "I don't think so at all," she replied. "But would you allow me to paint this one?"

She held it up to him.

"If you wish."

She smiled at him, and he was delighted at being the one who had made her do so. She climbed off the bed and tucked his drawing behind the painting of the woman with child, then turned back to face him. "So can I assume you wish to draw me naked?"

"Yes. I didn't want to discuss such a notion with you where anyone might hear. And then, well, you know what happened."

"Why me?" she asked.

"Because you are the most stunning, beautiful woman I have ever seen." It wasn't just for that reason he wished to draw her. There was something about her, some sort of connection that was different, and he desperately wanted to see how that translated to the page.

"Theo." His name whispered on her full lips did nothing to dissuade him from the notion that she was indeed the most perfect woman who walked the earth. Aphrodite herself would be put to shame.

"I shall understand if you decline." He hoped she wouldn't. Now that he had seen her naked, it only made him want to draw her more.

She stood before him bare, and the proximity of his siren almost made him want to drop the whole idea of drawing her and pull her back onto the bed.

"What about what occurred between us?" she asked.

"Nothing like that ever has to occur again, unless you wish for it to," he replied. "I didn't intend for it, but I'm not sorry it happened. I hope you aren't either."

"Of course not," she said quickly. "I'm afraid I might want more from you. Does that make me a wanton?"

"Not at all. Given neither of us delights in the prospect of marriage," he said, "perhaps we can enjoy each other while we are here." How could he offer to use an innocent for pleasure? He was playing with the hottest of fires and he merely spread his arms and walked head first into the flames.

She laughed. "I think that would be agreeable." He wasn't sure if he should be surprised that she agreed, but he only knew he wasn't strong enough to change his mind.

"And does that mean you might allow me to draw you then?"

She nodded. "When shall we begin?"

Chapter 6

"How about now?"

"Now?" She wanted him to draw her, but she thought she might need a while longer to get more comfortable with the idea.

"Why not? You are already naked, and we can light a few more candles. I'll sketch for a while and then I'll do something for you to help you sleep." His expression was even more mischievous in the light of the candles.

Being on display for him would be thrilling—and intimidating. She hadn't always felt comfortable in her own skin, especially with a body so different from the other ladies, and one that received such ridicule from those very same ladies. But with Theo, she didn't feel the urge to cover herself. She believed him when he said she was perfect, and the confidence his words gave her was intoxicating.

"Where do you want me?"

He laughed. "What a question, with many different answers. We shall keep it focused on art for the time being." He smirked at her.

Theo grabbed her hand and pulled her over to the settee. "Sit down here and lean back against the armrest."

She did as he said. "Turn on your side a bit so you face me more," he instructed.

Her elbow was underneath her, and he positioned her free arm to lie on her side. He moved her top leg so that her foot rested flat on the settee with her knee in the air, leaving her core open and bare to him.

"Beautiful," he said. "May I release your hair?"

She nodded, and he removed the ribbon and shook her hair loose from her plait. The sensation of him running his fingers through her hair heated her entire body. He positioned her hair to frame her shoulders.

He drew a deep breath and then swallowed hard. "It is going to take every ounce of my honor not to beg at your feet for you to give me your virginity, Jules. I only tell you this, so you always know how desirable you are."

She knew her neck and cheeks were flushed and would be a deep crimson from his words. Her cunt was already wet and aching for him to touch her again.

As if he heard her body's silent pleas, he leaned his head down between her legs and inserted his tongue inside of her and then ran it up to circle her delicate nub. She fought to remain in the position he put her in. "Yes, Theo," she moaned.

He pulled back and grinned at her. "That will give you something to think about while you lie there."

She noticed his cock was fully erect, so he wasn't unaffected by the action, which gave her a bit of satisfaction from him teasing her.

He lit a few more candles and positioned them on the tables that were at each end of the settee. The room was much brighter with the additional candles. He added a log to the fire and stoked it, reviving the roaring flames and casting dancing flickers of light within the chamber.

"There," he said. "I believe I shall begin."

She shivered, watching his eyes as he gazed at her. He sat in a chair across from her, still nude himself, holding a tablet with a parchment and a charcoal in hand. She longed to brush back some of the hair that fell across his handsome forehead as he began making his first marks with the charcoal.

She found that she loved watching him work. He appeared peaceful and content, the most himself and comfortable in his element she'd seen. Her heart pounded in her chest, and she did her best to ignore it. It wouldn't do at all to develop any actual feelings for him beyond friendship.

He was a rake unready to settle down in marriage, and she wasn't certain she wished to give up her freedom. But something about him made her question all of her resolve the longer she spent with him.

Juliet told herself she was just responding to the physical intimacy between them and that she desired to experience so much more of it. Besides, they were clearly comfortable in each other's presence, given the ease with which they adapted to their mutual state of nudity.

"Are you comfortable?" he asked, seeming to notice that her thoughts had drifted.

"Quite."

He smiled at her, and it was a smile that would have made her knees buckle if she had been standing. It was soft and sweet as if he found her to be the most precious thing in the world. Which was preposterous. He was a rake and had bedded many women. Counting the number of naked drawings he had would only be the start of his many conquests.

He knew how to entice women and lure them into his sphere. But she couldn't help but feel that something was different between them, even if he was a notorious rake. Perhaps that was a foolish notion. Of course it was. What was she thinking?

Theo continued to draw. Juliet wasn't even sure how long she sat propped up on the settee on display for him, but she enjoyed every bit of it. She loved the way her skin heated when his eyes gazed at her. She loved the way he licked and bit his lip while he made marks and lines with his charcoals. Every so often, he'd catch her gaze, and he'd flash her that heart-stopping smile.

He set his charcoals down and looked at his parchment, his expression indicating that he was pleased with what he had drawn. "Would you like to see?" he asked.

"Very much so." She was also nervous, wondering how he saw her.

He waved her towards him, and she shifted to stand and moved closer to his chair. He turned the parchment where she could see, and tears formed at the corners of her eyes. "This is beautiful, Theo."

"*You* are beautiful, Jules."

He must quit saying such things. She liked them far too much. She liked him far too much.

"Surely you enhanced some things."

He shook his head. "I drew you exactly as I see you. The perfect woman captured on parchment."

"We are beyond the need for flattery, Theo," she teased before becoming serious again. "You are so talented." He truly was, even if he doubted his ability.

He appeared touched and relieved by her compliment. "I assure you, it isn't hollow flattery, and thank you. That means a lot coming from you."

He tucked the parchment and tablet into his satchel and set it on the floor beside the chair. He clasped her bottom and pulled her against him, bringing his tongue back to her heat. Theo licked along the seam of her sex, and she released a low moan. "Are you still feeling a bit wanton?" he asked, pulling back to look up at her.

"Very much so." She wanted so much more of what she knew he could give her. And she only wanted him to be the one to do so.

He stood from his chair and pulled her into his arms. "Good, because I find I very much want to lick you until you come."

Her knees buckled from his words, and she might have fallen on him if he hadn't been holding her.

Unexpectedly, he pressed his lips to hers. She had never been kissed before, and the sensation of his lips against hers caused an electricity with an intensity she had never experienced. Juliet parted her lips in surprise, and he swept his tongue inside of her mouth. She pressed her whole body tighter against him when his tongue massaged hers. Kissing him was quickly becoming one of her favorite things.

He swept her up, cradling her in his arms without breaking their kiss. She wrapped her arms around his neck and fervently returned his kiss as he carried her to the bed and placed her down on it, then crawled into bed with her.

Theo pulled back. "Come up on your knees," he said, shifting to lie on his back.

Juliet did as he said, and on her knees beside him, she memorized every detail about what he looked like lying in her bed. His cock stood proudly, protruding from a dark nest of curls, and she noticed wetness at the tip. Feeling bold and recalling everything Eliza had told her about coupling with a man, she leaned down and licked the head of his member. She took the full head into her mouth and sucked, smiling around his shaft when he groaned.

"Jules, you don't have to…" his voice trailed off when she took more of him into her mouth, sucking her way further down the base. "Fuck," he moaned.

She pulled back. "What was that?" she asked, giving him a sweet, innocent smile. She was already addicted to making him respond and react to her thus.

He pulled at her thigh. "Put your knees on either side of my head," he commanded. "At least let me lick your sweet cunt if you wish to swallow my cock."

She was practically dripping from his words and shifted so she hovered herself over his face. He spread her knees wider so she was practically seated on him.

He licked her once from the start of her folds to her wet core. "I will tell you before I spend," he said before he resumed licking and teasing. She braced herself with her hands on each side of him, rocking with the movement of his tongue. She was quite certain there was nothing in the world that felt better than what he was doing to her.

She lowered herself so she rested her front to his, perfectly lined up to take his cock into her mouth again. She sucked from the head to the shaft, licking and tasting to match the intensity of what his wicked tongue was doing to her. Sucking him made it all even more intense, especially when he bucked his hips, moving himself in and out of her mouth.

He spread the cheeks of her arse and shifted his tongue from inside of her to run up to her untouched hole. Eliza had told her how she enjoyed the attention there, and Juliet had never thought it possible to be as delightful as it was.

"Will you let me draw you from behind? Bent over and so wet?" he asked, then resumed swirling his tongue in that most forbidden place, pushing it inside of her to stretch it just slightly.

"Yes," she moaned before taking him all the way to the back of her throat again.

He thrust into her mouth and shifted his tongue to lick and flick her nub, slipping two fingers inside of her. She moved her hips, rocking against his movements. He pressed his thumb to the hole of her arse, massaging it while he continued working his fingers and tongue. Unable to hold back any longer, she rocked on his face and moaned around his cock when she came. She sucked hard after she rode the intensity of her orgasm.

"Jules, I'm going to…" He tried to encourage her to stop, but she sucked him harder. He groaned and her mouth filled with the warmth of his seed, and she swallowed it down, unrelenting so that she pulled every bit of his climax from him. It was salty on her tongue, and she relished the feeling that she had been the one to elicit the response from him.

He licked her one more time and then she moved herself from atop him and shifted to lie beside him on the bed, their heads on adjacent pillows. Theo turned his head to look at her and she met his gaze, both of them smiling at each other. She felt no awkwardness or embarrassment, only satisfaction and contentment with the man beside her.

"Are you certain you haven't done that before?" he asked, his tone half jest and half serious.

"Never," she replied. "I have touched myself while imagining what it would be like, though. The reality is far better."

He reached for the blankets and pulled them over them, turning on his side to face her. She did the same, leaving only a few inches between them.

"Do I get to visit you tomorrow night to sketch you again?" he asked.

"I'd be disappointed if you didn't." That was the truth. She'd be disappointed if he didn't do other things as well.

He laughed. "Does that mean you enjoy being my muse?"

"Well, it comes with perks," she said.

The candles had tapered out and the fire was reduced to embers, so the room became dark, only the light of the moon shining across one side of the bed.

"Tell me about when you first started painting," he said. His voice was tender and genuine, and she was tempted to pluck her heart from her chest and hand it to him.

"My mother loved to paint, and I used to watch her. She would allow me to use some of her paints and brushes to try them out for myself. After she passed, I began painting to feel closer to her, and then I found it to be something I couldn't live without."

"That is much like me and drawing. I would draw with chalk instead of working on my letters."

"What made you start drawing naked women?" She didn't do so to judge him in the slightest, just wished to understand him better.

She could see the wide grin on his face in the moonlight.

"There is nothing more beautiful than the female form. I felt like if I could capture the essence of the female form, then I would be a skilled sketch artist."

"And have you done so?"

He reached out and brushed her hair away from her face. "Not until tonight."

Her breath caught, and she swallowed hard, attempting to stop herself from reading too much into his words. He was speaking of art, not feelings. Their arrangement was one of mutual intrigue, and she would do well to remember that.

She was at a loss for words and just watched him. They lay quietly together in the dark. His eyes drifted closed, and even though she knew she should wake him so he could return to his chamber, she threw caution to the wind and allowed hers to do the same.

The next morning, Juliet blinked her eyes open. The scent of sandalwood infiltrated her senses and the weight of something across her midsection pulled her focus. Theo lay beside her, sleeping peacefully, and his arm had made its way around her in the night. There was something more intimate about that moment than anything they had experienced together thus far.

The room was bright from the daylight breaking the horizon. It was only a matter of time before Bess would knock on her door to help her ready herself for the day.

Brushing the hair off his forehead, she took in all of his masculine features. The chiseled lines of his face relaxed from sleep. She thought he was even more handsome seeing him that way, and she had already acknowledged he was the most handsome man she had ever seen.

She drew a deep breath and reminded herself not to lose her heart to him. He would never marry her, nor did she have the desire to marry. At least she didn't believe she did, and not without love. She could only take what was offered during the house party and likely never see him again, unless he attended society entertainments. The notion of parting from him caused her throat to grow tight.

"Something the matter, Jules?" he asked, his voice gravelly. "I didn't mean to fall asleep."

"Not at all," she lied. "But you will have to depart soon if we are to avoid being caught."

He leaned forward and pressed a soft kiss on her lips, then shifted her beneath him so he hovered over her. "Not until I've broken my fast."

Theo kissed his way to her breasts and drew her nipple into his mouth, sucking the tight bud, eliciting a string of moans from her lips. He continued his journey down her body until he was positioned between her legs.

He lifted her legs so that they rested over his shoulders, giving him full access to her most private place. He licked and sucked her nub, then slid two fingers inside of her already-wet sheath. She arched her back and clasped his head, holding him where she wanted him.

"Theo," she moaned in a low whisper.

He moved his fingers within her, pulling them out and inserting them again. He replaced his fingers with his tongue and shifted a single finger lower, teasing the opening of her arse. He worked his finger inside the tight hole, pushing his finger further inside each time he withdrew and entered her again.

The sensation was so intense she rocked harder against him. In a matter of moments from his continued licking and sucking, in addition to his wicked finger inside of her arse, she shattered. She covered her mouth to muffle her moans. He removed his finger and used both hands to spread her folds, lapping up the proof of her orgasm.

"So damn good," he said when he finished. He kissed the inside of her thigh and then shifted her legs to lie on the bed.

He removed himself from the bed, and she watched him dress himself, sated and unable to move. Theo grabbed his satchel and then turned to face her. "I shall see you in the breakfast room. Although the offerings will be lacking compared to my first course."

She just shook her head and rolled her eyes at him. He was far too much of a flirt, and it was obvious why he was popular for his prowess.

He winked at her and then poked his head out the door before departing.

She couldn't help but wonder what it would be like to feel him inside of her. His words indicated he wished to do so. Perhaps if she told him she wished to as well, he might consider it. If she didn't intend to marry, what would it matter if she lost her virginity to the man she had grown to care for? Perhaps it would grow to love one day if she were willing to admit it, but she would be a fool to fall in love with a known rake.

Juliet rose from her bed and wrapped her dressing robe around her body. She positioned her easel and pulled out her newest painting from behind the others and moved it to the front. Needing to clear her head from all the thoughts and feelings for Theo, she did what always worked to distract herself. She painted.

Chapter 7

Theo had never slept so well in his life. Waking up to the jasmine that wafted from Juliet's hair and the feel of her warm, soft skin against his was almost more than his senses could bear. Not to mention that he could start his day by bringing her pleasure.

When he saw her again over the breakfast table, he hoped a pretty blush would reach her cheeks. As rakish as it was, he enjoyed the secret between them. Guilt nagged at him for a moment, thinking about the scandal that would ensue if they were to be caught, given that she was an innocent. Not that her mouth and the way she touched herself were all that innocent. Even so, he wasn't upholding any kind of gentlemanly principles for taking anything from her, but he couldn't help himself.

He wanted her. He wanted all of her. And worse, he wanted her to want him.

It was something he couldn't allow himself to imagine. Holding back from discovering what it would feel like to be inside of her would prove to be his biggest challenge yet. He reminded himself of the promise to his brother, and that he had kept the title free from scandal thus far and must continue to do so.

Since he seemed to enjoy torturing himself, he couldn't stop thinking about the drawing of her while his valet helped him to dress. It was the best drawing he had ever done. He didn't just capture her physical beauty; he captured the very essence of her. The feat he had been chasing for years. It was the first time he was satisfied with his work and could translate his vision onto the parchment.

When he wasn't thinking about how perfect she looked on paper drawn with charcoals, he was thinking about her lips and how he longed to kiss her again. He rarely kissed his bed partners, as it wasn't the type of connection he typically sought, but she was different. Everything about her spoke to him—perhaps spoke to his heart—and he'd had to taste her lips, to possess them, and once he did, he knew it wouldn't be the last time he did so.

His heart pounded, and he wouldn't allow himself to consider the cause. There weren't any feelings between them. They had the duration of the house party to enjoy each other's company. He would draw her as much as he could, and then he'd figure out where his art would take him since he'd achieved what he had been searching for.

Nowhere, most likely. He still had a title to protect, and the ton wouldn't accept him as an artist. It was the constant war he fought within himself, even though he already knew which side would be the victor.

Once he was dressed, Theo departed his chamber and made his way to the breakfast room. Like something akin to a lovesick schoolboy—although he wouldn't call it as such—he looked for Juliet as soon as he entered. When he fixed his gaze on his siren, his expression immediately turned to a scowl. Not that he should think of her as his to begin with, but pushing that aside, he scowled at Lord Duncan settled beside her at the table as if the odious man had triumphed over him.

Duncan said something to her, and then she released a laugh that sounded like the tinkling of bells. He tamped down the frustration building within him upon seeing her enjoying the company of another man, especially that one. He told himself he wasn't jealous. But hell, even if he was, didn't he have the right to be? His was the tongue between the lady's thighs not even an hour ago.

Theo made his selections from the sideboard, putting the food on his plate with short, annoyed movements. A couple of guests glanced his way when he clanked the serving utensils. He huffed and took a seat across from Juliet and Duncan, doing his best to do so without the dramatics he was inclined to invoke to call attention to his irritation.

At least she would be sure to see him and be aware of his presence seated before her. He took a bite of eggs and then looked up at her, finding that she stared back at him, confusion written across her expression. Theo gave her a tight smile, regretting it the moment he did. He tried to shift his visage to something friendlier, but when he smiled with his teeth, he knew he took it too far the other way. What was wrong with him?

"My lady," Duncan started, capturing her attention. "I do so look forward to shopping with you in the village today."

Why was she accompanying the man on the outing to the village? If the man thought he would get her alone, he was mistaken.

"It should be an enjoyable trip, my lord," she replied.

Theo seethed at her response and took a bite of his toast to distract himself. Never had he cared so much about a woman conversing with another man, and he didn't care to consider the notion any further.

Duncan droned on about his horses and all manner of topics that allowed him to list out the requirements he believed a lady might find desirable in a suitor. Juliet listened and paid him attention but didn't have the chance to say much in return. At the rate he was going, the man would be out of anything to discuss with her before they ever departed for the village, which would suit Theo just fine.

Once breakfast was over, the group departing for the village had gathered in the foyer so that carriages could convey them. Theo planted himself at Juliet's side, hoping to ensure that he would be in the same carriage as her.

To his frustration, Duncan had the same idea and wouldn't cease from sniffing around her skirts.

When it was their turn to board the next carriage, they both held out a hand to her to help her board the carriage. Theo fought the urge to roll his eyes at the mirth in her expression, watching their display. Even Theo had to admit that it was ridiculous, but he didn't want the man touching her. Even if it was only her gloved hand.

He knew enough about Duncan to know that the man was up to something, and that alone was enough of a reason he shouldn't be allowed in Juliet's presence. Theo might be a rake, even if he was beginning to question the accuracy of the label for himself, but he wouldn't marry a woman for her fortune and then dump her in the country once he had it. From what he knew of Duncan's gambling problems, he could only assume it was the end the man was playing at. Among other physical reasons the man would enjoy having her for a wife, which Theo would never allow. Another realization that he should ponder but pushed out of his mind.

"Camden," Duncan started, capturing his attention. "It appears Lady Lily is in need of an escort. I shall see to Lady Juliet if you can escort Lady Lily. We certainly want both beautiful ladies to be well attended."

One might compare Theo's reaction to that of a dog in the way he nearly growled through his teeth at the man. He stopped himself before it came to that. There was no polite way out of what the man suggested, unless he wished to offend the young lady, so he turned to Lady Lily, who stood behind them. "Might I help you into the carriage?"

She took his hand and grinned at him, but he didn't know her well enough to know if her interests were with another man. He hoped she hadn't set her cap at him, as it would be a fruitless endeavor given his aversion to marriage, or his willingness to give up Juliet. At present, his evenings for the rest of the house party would be spent in Juliet's chamber if she would have him. If not, he might stand guard outside her door, if only to ensure Duncan didn't get any ideas.

Theo almost thrashed the man for the way his eyes shifted to Juliet's arse when he handed her up before stepping back so that Theo could aid Lady Lily. Theo took the opportunity to board next, hoping he might sit beside Juliet, but was disappointed to find the ladies were already seated beside each other.

At least she would be across the carriage from Duncan, so he could live with that. Duncan boarded last and noted the seating arrangement. "Lady Lily, might you be willing to trade me seats? Camden and I are both large men and might find it difficult to share a seat."

It took every ounce of Theo's control to keep from reacting. He flexed his hands and formed tight fists. It was looking increasingly more likely that he'd throw a punch at some point that day. The man kept getting the better of him and it was dratted annoying. Of course the chit did as he asked and looked all too content to sit beside him.

He glanced at Juliet, and she offered him a small smile. He wasn't certain if she welcomed the man's attention, but if either of them thought he wouldn't be on their heels for the entire outing, they had another thing coming.

Theo expected Duncan to spout mindless chatter at Juliet again, but surprisingly, he spoke to Lady Lily instead.

"So, my lady, you just had your first season, is that right?"

"Yes, my lord," she replied. She was the daughter of the Earl of Fairfax. Her father was quite wealthy, and her dowry rivaled that of most debutantes, so the man hoped for an advantageous match for his daughter. At least that was what Theo had heard at his club. Theo figured that alone would have already seen her wed, even if she was a bit on the bookish, wallflower side. Perhaps Duncan would consider such a bride and leave Juliet alone. Although, he wasn't sure he would wish that on the poor lady.

"How fortuitous," Duncan said. "My friend Camden here could use a kind young lady to settle down with."

Theo fisted his hand at his side where no one but perhaps Juliet could see from across the carriage. Would Duncan still call Theo his friend when Theo's fist connected with the man's nose? If the man thought he would orchestrate a way to get Theo to leave him alone with Juliet, he was mistaken. It was high time Theo took control of the situation.

"Actually," Theo started. "I am uncertain of my plans for the future, but perhaps the four of us will get to know each other better when we tour the village together. What a merry group we will all make!" He mustered the most excitement he could. At least he wouldn't hurt the chit's feelings, and it would make it harder for Duncan to elude him.

"That would be lovely," Juliet said, offering him a knowing smile. A bit of tension released from his shoulders from her response. It appeared she didn't wish to be alone with the man, either. Based on the scowl Duncan gave him, he wasn't as thrilled with the suggestion just as Theo might have expected.

Duncan attempted to hide his frustration and refocused his attention on Juliet. "Did I hear that Lady Eliza has departed the party with Craven?"

Juliet beamed and Theo's heart pumped a steady rhythm at the sincere joy that radiated from her for her friend. "You did, my lord. They were childhood sweethearts and the party brought them together. They shall be wed and set up in their home well before the party ends, I wager."

"Well, good for them," Duncan said, almost sounding sincere. "Although, I do believe Irvine is licking his wounds from losing his chance with the lady. He stayed back at the house."

Juliet shrugged. "I can't help but feel anything but happiness for my dearest friend. She and Craven are a love match."

Juliet glanced out the window, and Theo thought he saw Duncan roll his eyes where she couldn't see. So at least that confirmed what Theo suspected, and love wasn't the emotion at the center of Duncan's motivations. Just as he had suspected.

When the carriage arrived in the village, a footman opened the door and handed each of the ladies down. Theo was left alone in the carriage with Duncan.

"Stay out of my way," Duncan warned before exiting the carriage.

Theo hurried to remove himself from the carriage. He knew Duncan would already have Juliet on his arm, but at least he could ensure he stayed with them.

Grumbling to himself, he extended his arm to Lady Lily, and he urged them to catch up to Juliet and Duncan.

"My lord," Lady Lily said from beside him, "I don't recall seeing you at any of the events this season."

He tried to pay attention to what she said. "What? Oh, I rarely attend those events." They needed to pick up the pace to stay on their heels.

"I see. Based on your current ire directed at Lord Duncan, can I assume that your heart belongs to Lady Juliet?"

At that, he spun his head towards her. "No, of course not." His heart didn't belong to anyone, nor would it ever. The notion was almost laughable.

She giggled, and it annoyed him since her expression was one of disbelief. "Are you certain?"

"Quite," he ground out. "She has become my friend of sorts, and I don't want her taken in by him," he said, nodding towards Duncan.

"I see. He does certainly seem to be trying hard. Too hard."

Theo released a hearty laugh at that. "Indeed. So I take it you don't find yourself interested in the man?"

She scrunched her nose. "Not at all. My father hopes that Lord Knox will ask for me."

The pair finally caught up to Lord Duncan and Juliet, following them as they strolled through one of the outdoor markets. Lady Lily stopped to look at some quills on display, and Theo stopped with her.

"My lady, I have to ask. Why didn't Knox attend with you today?"

"He wasn't feeling well and is resting from what I was told," she replied. "Although I'm uncertain if we shall suit. But my father is pushing the match. He says the earl has expressed interest."

"Hopefully, you will get to make the choice for yourself. Marriage is forever. That seems an awfully long time to be shackled to someone you don't wish to be." Theo glanced at Juliet, and something gnawed at his insides at the way she laughed at something Duncan said to her. The man's lips were far too close to her ear. Theo's entire body tensed, and his jaw set in a firm line, watching them.

"I quite agree, my lord. I am to spend this house party getting to know him better, and perhaps some of the other guests."

Duncan had moved his lips away from Juliet, and Theo did his best to refocus on his conversation with Lady Lily, uncertain if he had heard everything she had said. "I have heard nothing that is concerning regarding his behavior, if that is what you worry about. He isn't known to gamble or to frequent brothels."

She paid for the quill she held in her hands. "Thank you. That is helpful. I don't feel like I know him well at all. Perhaps the next few days in his company will give me more to go on."

"I wish you luck in your endeavor." At least she wasn't interested in him, nor Duncan. She seemed like far too kind of a lady to get snared by such a snake.

"Thank you," she replied. "I wish you luck in yours." She nodded towards Juliet.

He shook his head, starting to question what he had just thought about her being kind. "I told you already…"

"I know what you told me. And not that you asked for it, but my advice is that you quit pushing aside whatever it is you feel. You are merely lying to yourself."

Theo contemplated what the young miss said. He was certainly attracted to Juliet. He thought of her constantly and wished to be near her as often as he could. They both shared a love of the arts. She supported him, inspired him even.

He had to marry eventually, didn't he? Perhaps he should contemplate marriage as he promised his brother he would keep the title respectable and their tenants provided for. That would include marrying and providing an heir. The thought of marrying typically filled him with dread and would cause him to run as far as he could in the other direction, but all he had done thus far was try to get Juliet closer to him. The thought of marrying her didn't scare him, and that realization brought on the fear.

"Perhaps you are onto something, my lady."

He watched Juliet, and he found he could easily imagine waking up to her every day. The realization sent a shiver of unease through his spine and his heart beat so rapidly that he almost placed his hand over it.

If he didn't marry her, what then? He tried to picture what life would be like without her in it. What it would mean when they left the house party. He may never see her again, other than perhaps across a crowded ballroom, if he forced himself to attend. His stomach knotted and reeled from the realization of such a future.

Theo had much to think about. He owed it to himself, to both of them, to figure out his mind…and his heart. He needed to draw, to lose himself in his art. A wide grin played on his lips when an idea formed.

"Lady Lily, might you be willing to let me draw you when we return?"

Chapter 8

The trip to the village was an engaging distraction from being inside the house, but Juliet was glad to be back and spent the afternoon working on one of her paintings. She wished to finish it so that she could show it to Theo. She laughed to herself, recalling how he didn't seem to enjoy the trip to town at all. Duncan needled him for much of the trip. It wasn't good form, but Juliet couldn't blame the man for trying. It was clear Lord Duncan had hoped to catch her interest.

She found Duncan to be nice enough, but he tried too hard, which meant he likely had some ulterior motive. Besides, she feared her heart already belonged to Theo. She sighed at allowing herself to admit to the feelings. Theo had no intention of marrying, and if his art was any indication, he wouldn't be a faithful husband if he should ever take a wife. Warring with herself, she couldn't let herself forget her plans for the art gallery, which had been her dream.

Juliet shook off her thoughts and resumed painting. She wanted to get the colors just right. The afternoon light in her room was perfect, and she didn't wish to waste a single minute of it.

After painting for hours, Bess entered to help her dress. Once she was dressed and ready for dinner, she made her way to the salon. She wished Eliza was still in attendance. While she was delighted that her friend had reconciled with her love, she could benefit from her counsel. Eliza could help her sort through her feelings and make sense of things. Her friend would also tell her to guard her heart and prevent the pain and angst of giving it to a charming rake. But alas, she would have to reason things out on her own and do her best not to leave the house party with a broken heart.

Dinner was much the same as previous evenings. She wasn't seated near Theo, so she was at the mercy of Lord Duncan's conversation, mostly about himself. The tedious man had been seated on her left. Lord Knox was to her right, but he didn't seem too interested in striking up a conversation with her. Lady Preston sat across from her, caught up in conversation with the Duke of St. Albans.

Juliet had no choice but to spend the meal talking—or listening, rather—to Duncan. The man was funny in his own way. She wouldn't call him charismatic, but when he let a bit of sarcasm slip, she found she laughed at his jests. Beyond that, there wasn't much interesting or sincere about him.

Once everyone had finished their meal, the ladies retired to the salon. She chatted with Lady Preston and Lady Lily until the gentlemen joined. Lord Duncan came directly to Juliet and extended his arm to her.

"Might we take in the night air for a few moments?" he asked.

She placed her hand in the crook of his arm. "For a few moments, my lord." Juliet glanced around the room and noticed Theo chatting with Lady Lily. She fought the irritation that the pair seemed to have formed a friendship of sorts. At least she hoped that was all it was. They seemed to have been amiable to each other when they were in the village.

Juliet allowed Lord Duncan to lead her to the terrace, but something didn't quite feel right, and she knew she didn't wish to be alone with the man.

"It's a nice night out," he said, looking up at the sky.

"Indeed, only a bit chilly." Perhaps if she were cold, it would hasten her return to the salon with the other guests.

Lord Duncan turned to her. He brushed his knuckles against her cheek and caught her gaze. She didn't like his touch, or the dark look in his eyes. Contemplating what to do, as she would not let the man attempt to kiss her, her eyes darted to a figure nearby.

Over the man's shoulder, she saw Theo standing in the doorway, clenching his fists. She wanted to call out to him, tell him to come back and take her into his arms, to help rid her of Lord Duncan, but he turned and left.

Duncan began to lower his head, and she knew she must stop him.

"I find I am quite cold and must return inside," she said, hurrying away from him before he might grab her to pull her back. As her body raced away from Lord Duncan, her heart hurried after Theo.

She didn't see him in the salon and quickly continued towards the staircase. He was almost to the top of the stairs when she reached the landing at the bottom. "Theo," she called out to him.

He stopped but didn't turn around.

"Theo, please."

He turned to face her, and she hurried up the stairs to where he stood. There was no indication that he would speak as he stared at her. A hurt expression marred his handsome face.

"That wasn't what it looked like." She stepped closer to where they almost touched.

"Oh? It wasn't you on the terrace with a gentleman who was most certainly about to kiss you?"

She shifted on her feet. "Please come to my chamber. Give me a few moments to send Bess away for the evening, and then please come."

"I'm not certain I should."

She couldn't allow him to believe she would have kissed anyone but him. Not that she was certain he would offer her the same courtesy, but he was clearly upset by the notion, and she cared far too much about him to allow him to think differently.

"Please, Theo," she pleaded, taking his hand in hers. She was glad he didn't pull it away, at least. "I wish to speak with you, and it must be in private." She glanced behind them to confirm that no one should approach and find them alone together on the dark staircase.

"Very well," he said, but he didn't seem sure it was the right choice. "I shall be there in a quarter hour, assuming no one is moving about in the hallway."

"Thank you, Theo," she said, squeezing his hand before releasing it. She hurried away to her chamber. Once inside, she was pleased to see Bess waiting for her. Juliet had her maid help her into a night rail and then brush and plait her hair. She sent her away for the evening and waited.

Juliet paced her room, hoping Theo would arrive as he said he would. Then minutes, which felt like hours, later, her door opened, and she released a long breath when he stepped through it and locked the door behind him.

"Theo." She sighed.

"You wished to speak with me." His tone was far colder than she would have expected, and she took a step back. He had been with countless women. Why should he care if a gentleman had a mind to kiss her?

"Why are you so cross?"

"I'm not."

Well, if the cutting edge of his tone was any indication, that was surely a lie.

"Theo, I wasn't going to allow Lord Duncan to kiss me. I don't want him to kiss me. Ever."

"Is that so?" His tone was only slightly less irritated than before.

She took a few steps closer to him. "I don't go around kissing men. I have only ever been kissed by you."

His shoulders relaxed a bit from her words, but he contemplated her. Almost as if he was at war with himself.

"But," she started again, "I am uncertain why it bothers you so. You have been with many women and will surely do so again once we both depart at the conclusion of the house party."

He closed the distance between them and cupped her face with his hands, then pulled her lips against his. Sweeping his tongue in her mouth, he kissed her as if he were fighting for the air he needed to breathe. He broke their kiss and placed hungry kisses along her jaw and neck.

"Theo," she moaned.

He stopped what he was doing and caught her gaze. They stared into each other's eyes for a few moments. It was the most intense, charged moment of her life. She wanted him desperately, but she also knew at that moment that she had fallen in love with him. She thought she might have read love in his expression, but it was most likely the weight of his desire. He owned every piece of her heart, and even if it made her the most foolish woman in England, she wanted him.

Being with him even once would be better than never having him at all.

"I want you," she whispered, still capturing his eyes with hers.

He opened his mouth as if he would say something and then closed it again. He swallowed hard, and she thought his eyes might have become glassy, but it was probably just the candlelight playing tricks on her.

"Are you certain?" he finally asked.

She nodded.

"You must say the words." He clasped her hands in his.

She squeezed his hands. "I am certain that I want you, Lord Theodore Camden, in every way." She had never spoken truer words.

Juliet knew she would marry him, if he asked, and have his children. Build a full, loving, passionate life with him. His was the face she wanted to see every day, the one she wanted to share in her excitement when she finished a painting, to ride their estates together, and cling to each other at night. She allowed herself to admit that she wanted it all, even if she was uncertain about admitting such a revelation to him.

She'd never thought she could want or trust a man as much as she did him, even if it was fast and she hadn't known him all that long, but she wanted such a life with him. If that made her mad, then so be it. Her more reasonable mind knew that it was a schoolgirl fantasy. Theo didn't want any of it other than what she offered him, but he could be hers for a while. And that would have to be enough.

He responded to her words by grasping the side of her night rail and pulling it over her head in a single fluid motion. He began working on the buttons of his shirt, while she released her hair so that it fell freely down her back.

She stepped against him and pushed his shirt off his shoulders once he finished with the last button, letting it fall to the floor. Juliet reached for his falls, but he wrapped his fingers around her wrist to halt her. "Not yet. I need to keep my wits about me."

Her thighs were already damp, and that she was the one driving him to a similar state only made her want him more. He kicked off his boots and took her lips again. Backing her towards the bed while he kissed her, he ran his hands along her sides and continued until he clasped her arse. He lifted her against him, and she wrapped her arms and legs around him. His bulge was hard, and she undulated against it as best as she could while he held her standing beside the bed.

He broke their kiss and rested his forehead on hers. "You are going to make it impossible for me to go slow for you. You are intoxicating."

"Don't hold yourself back. I just want you," she whispered.

He kissed her again, then laid her across the bed. She came up on her elbows and watched him unbutton his falls and push them to the floor. If she could live the rest of her life staring at him, she would.

Theo crawled onto the bed and hovered over her, his hard cock rubbing against her as if taunting her. He kissed her neck and worked his way to the globes of her breasts. He took one in his hand and massaged it before taking her nipple into his mouth.

"Theo," she moaned. "I need you."

He picked his head up and looked at her. "You shall have me, but you deserve to be cherished, and that is exactly what I am going to do." He lowered his head to her other breast and repeated the same attention to her tightened bud. Her wet heat throbbed, the anticipation almost unbearable. She tried to move against him, hoping part of him might rub against her and sate some of her need.

When that proved not to ease the ache, she attempted to move her hand between them. He captured her wrist just as she clasped his cock. He moved it over her head and pinned it to the bed. Before she could make another attempt with her other hand, he clasped that one, too, and joined it with her other hand. He pinned them together with his left hand.

"Eager, are we?"

"Theo," she whined.

"I am determined to make this good for you. It is going to hurt a bit your first time, and I want you to be so wet, and hot, and ready that perhaps it will ease the pain."

She knew she must be soaking the sheets already from how he drove her to distraction. "I am ready."

"Let me be the judge of that." He smirked at her. He shifted his right hand down her body, gently squeezing her hip before brushing his fingers between her legs. She arched her back when he did, pulling against where he pinned her wrists. The anticipation made the action feel more intense than it had ever felt before.

He kissed her, massaging her tongue with his, and rubbed her sensitive place in maddeningly slow circles. As he rocked her hips, she felt him smile against her lips. He raised his head to look into her eyes and shifted his hand lower. It was her turn to smirk when he slipped a finger into her heat and his eyes shuttered closed.

"I don't think you could be any more ready for me," he groaned. He opened his eyes again to look at her. "Tell me again, you are certain. I can lick you clean right now, and we needn't go any further."

She pushed her hips against him as much as she could. "I have never been more certain. You are the only man I shall ever want." She regretted her words, worried she would scare him away completely. He wasn't a man who wished to wed.

To her surprise, he responded by kissing her. He released her hands, and she wrapped her arms around his neck, holding him against her.

He placed his hands on either side of her head and positioned himself at her opening, the head of his cock just barely teasing her.

"I'll do my best to allow you to adjust. Let me know if it hurts."

She nodded, and he pushed himself inside of her, only an inch. He gradually entered her further, an inch at a time. He made one thrust, bringing with it a small rush of pain, and then he was completely inside of her, their bodies pressed together.

"Are you all right?" he asked, the concern evident in his expression.

Juliet nodded. "It only hurt for a moment. It's mostly gone now." She shifted her hips. "I need something."

Theo grinned at her and placed several kisses along her jaw. He withdrew, and she clasped him tighter, hoping he would not leave. Then he thrust back inside of her, and she cried out. It was unlike anything she could have imagined, and that she was experiencing it with the man she loved only made it all the better.

"Wrap your legs around me," he whispered.

She did as he said, and when he thrust again, he entered her even deeper. When she closed her eyes, she almost believed she was flying. He continued moving within her in long, steady thrusts. Each one was more intense than the last and drove her closer to the edge of ecstasy.

"Eyes on me, beautiful," he said. "Do you like this?"

She opened her eyes and saw the tenderness in his expression. She cupped his cheek. "Nothing has ever felt better."

He thrust into her again. "I quite agree."

She whimpered, her heart melting into her insides. Theo quickened his pace. She gripped him tighter with her legs and dug her fingers into his back as she came even nearer to exploding beneath him.

Theo feathered kisses along her jaw until he reached her ear, taking her lobe between his teeth. His hot breath on her ear sent shivers throughout her body.

Brushing his lips across her ear, he whispered, "Come for me. Shatter around my cock and let me hear my name escape from your perfect lips." He shifted his mouth so that he kissed her again.

Everything in her body clenched tighter around him when he thrust into her again and pushed her over the cliff of something she didn't know could be so wonderful, and she indeed moaned his name as she rocked and shook from the longest climax she had ever experienced. Theo leaned down again and kissed her, swallowing the moans as she rode each and every second of unbridled bliss.

When she stilled, he thrust into her one more time before removing himself, and the warmth of his seed covered her stomach. He ground out her name as he spilled every drop, and she enjoyed watching his face when he did so.

He drew in a few breaths, still holding himself above her before he opened his eyes and caught her gaze again. The smile he gave her made her swallow hard and captured her breath. "Don't move," he said.

When he shifted himself off the bed, she immediately felt the loss of him. The cool night air made her more aware of how vulnerable and exposed she was to him, in more ways than just her naked body.

He returned with a cool, damp cloth and wiped between her legs, and then wiped her stomach clean. All the evidence and proof of what they shared was gone, at least gone from her body. The realization gnawed at her. How could she think that being with him in that way once would ever be enough? She schooled her features when he climbed back into the bed.

He placed himself in the same spot he had slept in the previous evening and reached for her hand, then pulled her towards him. Theo lay on his back and settled her to lie against him, his arms wrapped around her. Their legs intertwined and she draped her arm across his waist. She rested her head on his chest, thankful that he couldn't see her face since she knew she might cry at any moment.

The silence hung between them for a few moments until he finally spoke. "I have never held another this way before."

His words pushed her over the edge, and a tear escaped. She discreetly brushed it away so he wouldn't see. She couldn't speak, but also she wasn't certain he expected a response.

"The mere notion of Duncan's lips touching yours had me ready to thrash the man." He kissed the top of her head, and the gesture touched her heart. "I've never felt that way about anyone before."

She nodded against him.

He hooked his finger under her chin and tilted her head up towards him. "I believe you have ruined me, and I shall never get enough of you."

She smiled at his words, still not certain she should get her hopes up for a deeper meaning behind them. Juliet swallowed hard, contemplating how to respond.

"I quite agree," she replied, fighting away her tears and smiling at him with all the love she felt. She hoped he might read her expression and know without needing to speak the words.

He released her chin and stroked her back, moving his fingers lazily across her skin as they lay there together. The scene was so intimate and intense, and she longed for them to be just as they were every night of her life.

She closed her eyes and allowed herself to dream of such a life, as dreams may be the only place where it would be true.

Chapter 9

Theo lay in bed with Juliet in his arms and was more content than he had ever been, and it was all because fate saw fit to bring them together. He had never imagined that love would strike him and that he would welcome it as much as he had. Once he admitted to himself that he was in love with her, everything fell into place from there. He had decided already that he could never let her part from him. He needed her in his life, in her rightful place at his side.

He drew Lady Lily that afternoon when Juliet retired to her room to paint. Theo had never drawn a woman clothed before, and he wanted to prove to himself that his talent didn't require his models to be naked and bare before him. Although, he would still draw Juliet in every position imaginable, but that was just for them.

While he drew, he sorted through his feelings, which he knew were strong. It took him a while to identify them because he had never before felt as such. The more he drew, the clearer it became that Juliet was the woman for him. It was madness, and it had only been a couple of days, but didn't someone say that love moved swiftly? It did, indeed.

He hadn't decided when he would tell her as he didn't wish to scare her away. But when he saw that bounder Duncan attempt to touch her and that she even went on the terrace with the blackguard to begin with, he'd lost all rational thought. His first inclination had been to toss the man over the railing of the terrace, but if she wanted the man, who was he to impede what she wanted? He loved her that much, so he walked away.

Theo glanced down at the top of Juliet's head on his chest. She was fast asleep, her breathing even and steady. The sound was almost melodic, and he only hoped he'd get to listen to that song every night in their shared chamber. He would never sleep apart from her, that was for certain. A realization that was laughable considering his thoughts on the matter only a couple of days ago.

He had wanted to tell her he loved her after they'd made love. He smiled to himself, knowing that was exactly what they did. It had never been like that before, and he finally understood the difference. He knew she had nothing to compare it to, but he hoped her heart knew. She was it for him. There would never be another.

Telling her so while they were both caught up in the heat of what they experienced seemed just a bit too cliché. He wanted her to know that his feelings for her weren't just because of the intimacy between them, but were what drove their passion to the brink of madness. He believed, hoped rather, she might feel the same way, but he'd have to muster up the courage to ask.

He always figured that if he ever married, it would be because he accepted his fate to continue the line for the title, and that the woman would accept him so that she could be a marchioness. Love wouldn't have played any part in it. Now that he needed her the same way he needed water and air to survive, asking her to marry him left him nervous and unable to calm himself.

Suddenly, he knew what he must do. He shifted her off him and onto her pillow. She stirred in the transition, and he rubbed her back again. He kissed her brow. "Go back to sleep, sweetheart," he whispered. "I'm here."

Theo continued rubbing her back until her breath evened out again and he knew she was back asleep. He carefully shifted himself out of the bed and turned to watch and make sure she remained asleep. Once convinced she wouldn't awaken, he quietly went to her easel where her supplies were. He took out a blank piece of paper and some of the charcoals she used to sketch her paintings.

He moved a chair closer to the bed and lit a candle so he could see her while he worked. He glanced up every so often and his heart flipped at the sight of her sleeping so peacefully. Theo looked back at his drawing, urging himself to complete it so he could get back in bed with her and enjoy at least a few hours of sleep beside the woman he loved.

Once he finished his drawing, he smiled and assessed his work. It was perfect if he said so himself. He folded the paper and placed it beneath the pillow on his side of the bed. He blew out the candle and climbed back into bed with her. As soon as he settled back beside her, she nestled closer until she was back in his arms.

"Theo," she mumbled, not opening her eyes.

He stroked her hair, and she settled back into sleep. He held her tightly to him and closed his eyes, pushing aside his racing thoughts about what he would say to her in the morning so he might find sleep.

The next morning, the sun gleamed outside the window. Juliet was in the same place with her head on his chest, her long, wavy hair splayed out behind her. He allowed himself to imagine what a life waking up every morning with her in his arms would be like. If only she would accept him.

His brother would be proud of him. He would marry, and he would have the perfect marchioness at his side to help manage the estate and see to their tenants. He would need to be there to ensure things ran as his brother wanted, and Juliet could still paint to her heart's content in the countryside. Theo thought he might even have a room completely redesigned to be her painting studio as a wedding gift.

She stirred against him, and the movement of her skin against his caused his cock to stir. He tamped down his desire as he needed her to know that his love was true and wasn't because of how much he loved to touch and taste her—although he did love those things as well. Their physical compatibility was just a very pleasurable bonus.

Juliet looked up at him, and her mesmerizing grey eyes bore into him. Her lips curved into a sweet smile and his heart beat even faster.

"Good morning, beautiful," he said before placing a soft kiss on her lips.

"You don't have to work your charms, Theo. I have already allowed you into my bed," she returned, giggling.

Theo cupped her cheek, urging her to look at him. He couldn't have her believing that any of his words to her were mere attempts to take more from her. He didn't wish to take anything from her, but rather he wanted to give her everything. She had his body, of course, but she had his heart and soul as well.

"I mean every word I speak to you."

Her breath caught, and she contemplated him.

He reached beneath his pillow and found the piece of paper with his drawing from last night and handed it to her.

"What is this?" she asked, cautiously taking the paper into her hands.

"Open it." His body tensed, hopeful that all would go as planned. Once she saw it, there was no turning back.

She sat up, the sheet falling away from her and leaving her naked breasts exposed to him. He followed suit and sat up, scooting closer, so he sat beside her. Putting his arm around her and clasping her hip, he waited for her to unfold his drawing.

She looked up at him, a question in her eyes. He responded by nodding towards the paper.

Juliet drew a deep breath and unfolded it. He watched her expression. It went from surprise to joy, then confusion to her eyes welling with tears. He wasn't sure which of those emotions he most hoped to spark, but the combination of them all somehow left him on edge.

"Jules?"

She stared at the drawing. It was a sketch of her in a wedding dress. He had memorized her so well that he was proud of the likeness, especially doing without the best lighting. Beneath it, he had written his proposal. She looked up at him, confused, that being the emotion that seemed to win the battle.

When she didn't say anything, he broke the silence. "So will you marry me?"

She shook her head, and his heart became heavy in his chest.

"Theo," she whispered. "I don't want you to marry me because of—"

He pressed his finger to her lips.

"Jules, I finally let myself realize that my heart was lost to you yesterday when I had to watch you on that idiotic man's arm. I intended to tell you as much before I played the part of the jealous fool. I don't pretend to be perfect or even good enough for you, or to possibly believe that I won't make many mistakes in the coming years. All of which you can make me pay dearly for. But what I know is that I love you. I can't imagine a day of my life without you in it. That is the reason I ask for you to marry me, and for that reason alone."

Tears streamed down her cheeks, and she threw her arms around his neck.

"You must forgive me for not getting down on one knee, but I worried it would be rather awkward given that I am currently naked. I just didn't wish to wait any longer to ask you."

She hugged him tighter and nodded against his cheek.

"Not to be difficult, but it would be helpful if you would give me a verbal answer, so I might be able to breathe again," he said before turning his head to kiss her temple.

She pulled away from him and caught his gaze. "Yes, Theo. I will marry you."

He released an audible sigh. "I suppose I must ask your father before we can consider ourselves officially betrothed since you haven't reached your age of majority." He hadn't considered that until that moment, and his nerves returned. He didn't know the earl well and, given Theo's reputation, it was quite possible the man wouldn't find him to be a suitable match for his daughter.

He must have worn his concern on his face because Jules used her thumb to smooth his brow.

"All will be well. Papa will approve the match. He wants me to be happy."

"I hope so. If only I hadn't lived such a rakehell life." What respectable father would choose such a man for his daughter?

She shook her head. "All your life experience has made you the man you are today. The man I love. You can't change the past, so we will focus only on our future together."

"I promise you, my love. Those days are behind me. You are the only woman for me for the rest of my days." He meant it, too. There was no one else who could ever compare to his siren.

"You'll convince Papa of the very same, and then we shall wed."

He clasped her hand and brought it to his lips. "I love you."

"I love you, too." She leaned close to him and brushed her lips against his.

Theo held her tight against him and swept his tongue across her bottom lip. She opened to him, and he pressed his tongue to hers. She returned his intensity, and their tongues mated while their hands wandered and explored.

A voice sounded from the hallway, which caught Theo's attention. "Sweetheart, I must go. We can't be caught with me naked in your bed, or your father is certain to hate me once he found out. I'd be meeting him at dawn."

"I would stand directly in front of you if he should do something so foolish."

He shook his head and then kissed her again. "No dueling grounds for my future wife."

Theo climbed from the bed and quickly donned his clothing. He was at least only half hard by that point, which aided in his ability to part from her. The visual of her angry father was effective at killing any notion he may have to say to hell with getting caught and then thoroughly bedding her that morning. But the same couldn't be said for later that evening.

Her lips formed a slight pout as she watched him button his shirt the rest of the way.

"Might you allow me to join you again this evening?" he asked, hoping that might make up for his quick departure.

"You needn't ask."

He walked back to the bed and leaned closer to give her a quick kiss.

"Don't agree to any entertainments today. We shall take a stroll in the gardens after breakfast and discuss our plans for me to speak with your father."

"I suppose we can't speak of our intended betrothal to the other guests until you have spoken with Papa," she said, frowning.

"It's probably for the best. We will want to ensure your papa doesn't think I have compromised his daughter." He winked at her.

She laughed. "Given how you had sworn off marriage before we met, perhaps I am the one who compromised you."

He brought his finger to his lips. "Well, that'll be our little secret. At least for now. Once your father has agreed, you can tell the world that you hold my heart in your hand."

Chapter 10

Juliet couldn't believe that she was going to marry at all, let alone marry the notorious Lord Camden. Theo. She wished Eliza were there so she'd have someone she could confide her news in before she burst. Her best friend would be delighted for her. Eliza would likely be married to Nick in a matter of days and could hopefully be there for her own wedding. A part of her was sad she would miss seeing Eliza marry the man she loved, but she understood they had been kept apart for far too long. They deserved to marry as soon as possible and make up for lost time.

It took all of Juliet's patience to suffer through conversation with Lord Duncan while seated at breakfast. Theo did the best he could to keep her engaged in conversation on her other side, but Lord Duncan wasn't taking the hint. She couldn't very well shout to the man that she was marrying Theo. Every time Duncan slipped into the conversation, forcing her to adhere to good manners and engage with him, she thought about Theo's hand on her thigh. He had slipped his hand to rest there, and she enjoyed his protective touch. She only hoped no one took notice that she sat just a bit closer to Theo than she did to Lord Duncan.

Although she would much rather tell the entire world and begin planning their future together. At least they could be afforded time alone together that they wouldn't have if she were back at home with Papa.

After breakfast, Theo escorted her away from the table, and they hurried out to the garden before Lord Duncan could follow and see where they went. Theo held her hand and pulled her along as she covered her mouth with her other hand to stifle her giggles.

Once alone deep in the garden, he tucked her hand in the crook of his arm, and they strolled along the path.

"If that man glanced at your chest one more time, I was going to plant him a facer right there in the breakfast room," Theo ground out.

Juliet laughed. "I am so used to it. And don't pretend you didn't do so the first time we met."

"I must apologize for my gender." He shook his head. "Besides, I am to be your husband, and you now grant me permission to look."

"Wouldn't the scandal sheets love to hear you now?" she said, giggling behind her hand.

"Once you are my wife, I don't give a whit if they speak of my fall from bachelorhood. As long as they only write kind things about my wife." He pulled her behind several tall hedges and placed several kisses along her lips and jaw. "I shall happily be under my wife's paw, among other things."

She waved him off, and they started walking again. Juliet glanced across the field and grinned when she noticed one of the gentlemen, seemingly the Duke of St. Albans, sneaking off beyond the gardens. Perhaps he was meeting one of the other ladies. Love was certainly in the air, it seemed.

There was a gazebo ahead with a bench. Theo led her to it and helped her to sit before seating himself next to her. "So do you think I should write to your father and have him attend us here? Or should we depart?"

"Allow me to think on that. I want to give us the best chance of success." Surely Papa would be happy she found love. "I don't think we should insult our hosts with another couple leaving their party."

He nodded. "Indeed. I shall defer to your recommendation on how to proceed. And when we are married, do you wish to go on a honeymoon trip, or would you like to settle into our home?"

"Do you have a home in Scotland?"

"I do, in fact," he replied, grinning at her.

She clasped her hands together. "Might we spend some time there? Mama was half Scottish and I've always wished to see the beautiful lands. I might even paint some of the views."

"If that is your wish, that is where we shall go. Perhaps I will do a bit of drawing."

"You don't draw landscapes, my love," she said, smirking at him.

He took one of her hands in his. "Aren't I fortunate that my muse will be on the journey with me? Besides, I would like to try my hand at drawing all manner of things."

"I look forward to seeing anything that you create." He was far more talented than he gave himself credit for. His work belonged in a gallery.

"Between the two of us, our walls shall be filled."

"That reminds me," she said. "Might we make some time to visit London at some point? I'd like to look for a place that would make for a good location for an art gallery."

He eyed her curiously. "What are you talking about?"

"I would like to open an art gallery, one that will also feature women's art. The galleries in town aren't as accepting of art that is done by women, particularly one from the *ton*, and I wish to change that. I want to display the talent of all." She was so excited to share her dream with Theo. With him at her side, it was sure to be a success.

"Jules, you can't be serious." Unfortunately, there wasn't a smile to be found on his handsome visage.

She leaned back slightly to assess his reaction. "I assure you, I am quite serious. It has been a dream of mine."

"We are titled. You will be the Marchioness of Camden. We will need to tend to the estates and see to our tenants' livelihoods. Involvement in such a scandalous endeavor would put our standing in society at risk."

"This from the man who frequently appeared in scandal sheets for his libertine lifestyle? Was that also for the benefit of your tenants?" She knew it was a low blow, but she questioned if she even knew the man. She had never expected him to react to her dream in that way.

He released a low growl, and she realized she had never seen him angry before. "Jules, that isn't fair, and you know it. They are not the same things."

"Because the *ton* will turn their head for a man who pursues whatever or whomever he wishes, while a woman is an outcast if she wishes to pursue anything besides pleasing her husband, bearing his children, and running his household." That was exactly why she had resigned herself never to take a husband. She should have known that no man—not even Theo—would support her dreams.

"I support your art, Jules. I would never want you to quit painting and doing things you love."

"As long as I do so in a way that doesn't jeopardize your place in society, is that correct?"

He ran his hand down his face. "We have responsibilities. We need our position in society to ensure that we maintain the profits for our estates and ensure our future for generations to come. Surely you can understand that? And besides, running a gallery in town would be a lot of work. We would need time to be at our country home."

"You don't think I understand how business works? You believe I am incapable of hiring staff and overseeing the management of such an endeavor?" He was playing every bit the part of the pompous man who believed he knew best, and she didn't care for it one bit.

"Jules, sweetheart, I never said that. But can't you see reason? This plan is nonsense."

She rose from her seat. "What is nonsense is my thinking that I could marry you."

He jumped up to face her. "You don't mean that."

"I can't marry you, Theo." Tears formed in her eyes. It would break her heart to lose him, but if he asked her to sacrifice her dreams, he wasn't who she thought he was.

"Why? Do you no longer love me now, just like that?" The hurt in his cracked voice almost broke her resolve.

She closed her eyes and drew a breath for strength before answering him. "Of course I love you. I probably always will. But you believe my dreams are nonsense, and I can't marry a man who wouldn't stand by me, regardless of what it might make other lords think of him for doing so."

"Jules, please don't do this," he pleaded, reaching for her hand, but she pulled it away. "Juliet, I love you."

"You love who you wish for me to be. But my mind is made up," she replied. "I wish you the best, my lord."

She hurried away, leaving him alone in the gazebo. She moved as quickly as she could, not wanting him to catch her and pull her into his arms. Juliet wasn't certain she would be strong enough to walk away from him if he did so.

Juliet fought the tears that were quickly blocking her vision. Once inside the house, she hurried up the stairs and into her chamber. She locked the door behind her, just in case the man followed her. She threw herself onto her bed and her body shook from the sobs that finally broke free. The pillow, which smelled like Theo from where he slept on it the night before, quickly became soaked with her tears.

After several minutes of crying, she calmed down and urged herself to sit up. Wiping her eyes, she drew in several deep breaths. With her heart broken into a million pieces, which would likely never mend, she rose and went to her easel. She pulled the drawing of the woman that Theo had done from its hiding place and started back to work at finishing it. She only hoped she might find some kind of joy, even if only slightly, with her paintbrush in hand. It was all she had left.

Chapter 11

Theo paced the gazebo. What in the hell had just happened? How could she abandon him and break his heart as if it were nothing? She said she loved him, but she walked away. He kicked a pebble. How had they gone from blissfully happy to agonizingly miserable in a matter of a few minutes? Wasn't finding love supposed to be a joyous, wonderful occasion? Didn't love conquer all or some shite? If heartbreak and misery were what he could expect, he wasn't certain he wished for any of it.

He left the gazebo and started back towards the house. Once he was back inside, he went to the salon, hoping he might find a tumbler of brandy. At least, in that regard, luck was on his side. He poured a glass and immediately drained all of it. Theo poured another and swirled it a few times before downing all the liquid again.

"You do realize it isn't even noon yet, my lord."

Theo spun around. "Lady Lily, shouldn't you be off with Lord Knox somewhere?" He wasn't in the mood for mindless chatter.

"He is supposed to meet me shortly. But you seem to be in a state."

He turned back to the sideboard and refilled his glass, then waved his hand as he spoke. "If rejected, miserable, or crushed are considered a 'state', then you are correct."

"Lady Juliet, I assume?"

He released a low growl. "The very one." This chit was too smart, and nosy, for her own good.

"What did you do?"

He turned back towards her and glared. How dare she blame him for what occurred? He had done nothing wrong. Had he? "Why do you assume it is *I* who did something?"

"Forgive me, my lord, I shouldn't have assumed. What has occurred?"

He nodded towards the terrace and then exited through the door, glass in hand. She understood his intention and followed him.

"The woman agreed to marry me and then dropped it on me how she wishes to open an art gallery. One that will feature women's art, regardless of their position in society."

He waited for her to react, expecting her to gasp or express some kind of shock. Clutch her necklace, perhaps? Every second that passed where she didn't only annoyed him further. "Well?" he finally asked.

"I'm still waiting to hear the problem."

He wanted to groan and storm off. Why was he even discussing this with her? More of his folly for the day.

"Surely you jest. A titled woman of society opening and running an art gallery? One where she will also feature her own art pieces and that of other women in society? The *ton* would never allow such a thing. It's nonsense."

Lady Lily sucked an intake of air. "Please tell me you didn't use those words with Lady Juliet."

"I spoke the truth."

She shook her head. "Foolish man."

"See here—" he started, but she cut him off.

"Lord Camden, you called your beloved's dreams nonsense. Can you not see how that might make her upset? Also, it isn't nonsense. I happen to believe she would garner a lot of support from the women, and in turn the men, who wish to keep their wives happy."

He clenched his fists. "I can't risk that. I made a promise to my—"

She held up her hand to silence him. "Don't explain it to me. If you have reason to be concerned, you must explain that to her. Then come to a resolution together. But keep your wits about you and don't diminish and belittle what she wants just because you are a man who believes he knows best."

"I don't…"

"You do, my lord. You all do. It isn't easy being a woman in a society where we are the property of the men in our lives. First our father and then our husband. So if you truly love her as you say you do, perhaps you might put yourself in her shoes and imagine how she might feel. That should help you come to an agreeable solution."

He groaned. The chit was right. She was far wiser than he wished to give her credit for. Even if he wasn't ready to accept the notion of the art gallery, he certainly couldn't leave things as they were. He loved Juliet too much to just let her walk away from him. Even if it stung his pride that she had done so.

"Thank you, Lady Lily. I shall think about what you said."

If he thought she was finished lecturing him, he was mistaken.

"These men you worry so much about appealing to are pompous arses who also believe they know best, and you think to blindly follow their expectations for you? You must ask yourself if their opinion of you matters more to you than that of Lady Juliet's."

He really hated how right she was and how no matter which way he looked at, he was the arse. Even if he had his reasons.

"I appreciate that you didn't hold back your sharp tongue, my lady. I wish your future husband the best of luck." He smirked, then gave her a small bow. "If you will excuse me, I must speak with her. I ask for you to keep this matter to yourself."

She flashed him an amused grin. "My lips are sealed."

Theo nodded and quickly took off, determined to go to Juliet and discuss everything with her and resolve things between them. He reached her door and tried the knob, finding it locked. He lightly rapped his knuckles on the door. There was no reply. He knocked harder.

"Yes?"

"Juliet, please let me in," he loudly whispered.

"I don't wish to speak to you right now."

He dropped his head into his hands, getting his wits about him before he took a running start at her door.

"Jules," he said softly. "I beg you to let me in. We can't leave things like this. I want to explain a few things, and I want to hear about your dreams. We can find a solution together. Please. I can't lose you."

He looked around and only hoped that no one would come across him begging at her door. Not because he cared if they knew he was a besotted fool, but because he didn't wish for a hint of scandal to force her to wed him. He wanted her as his wife because she longed for it as much as he did, and for no other reason.

The sound of the lock turning caught his attention. She cracked the door, then stepped aside so he could enter. He swept in and locked the door behind him.

"Thank you for letting me in, sweetheart." The first hurdle had been cleared.

"What is it you wish to say?"

She was prickly at best, so he'd have to tread carefully, or he'd quickly find himself being pushed back into the hall.

He drew a deep breath. "The reason I am concerned about the estates and preserving the title is because I promised my dear brother on his deathbed that I would do so."

Her expression softened, and he swallowed hard, forcing himself to continue.

"I should never have been the marquess. Thomas was born for the title. He was the responsible one, the one born to lead and born to ensure that the family name prospered." Theo drew another long breath, fighting back the emotion that always came when he thought of his beloved brother. "Thomas was my best friend, and all I had after our parents died. He should be here." He paused, swallowing hard so he could continue speaking. "But he made me promise I would do as he would. I have done my best, which isn't good enough. I hired the best staff to assist and do most of the work. I don't love the title or the responsibility, but I loved my brother, and I promised him."

His voice cracked on the last few words, and she closed the distance between them and took him into her arms.

"Theo," she whispered. "I had no idea. The expectations of that promise must weigh so heavily on you."

"I'll never be the marquess or even half the man he was."

She hugged him harder. "You shall never be your brother because you are Theo. You were always meant to be Theo. You can do the best you can for the people in your care and still be true to yourself. It's not fair for anyone to expect perfection from you."

If he wasn't already certain he loved her, her words would have sealed his fate. And he didn't have a single doubt of her love for him. He heard it in her words and how she supported him and loved him for who he truly was, even when she was upset with him.

He hugged her back, burying his face in her neck. Glancing up, he noticed his drawing on her easel behind her.

"Jules, that is incredible."

She released him and turned to see what he was looking at. "Well, a talented artist gave me the canvas. I just tried to see it through his eyes."

"This is what you are meant to do, my love. This is remarkable. It is almost exactly what I hoped to capture in the drawing, and you brought it to life."

"We make a good team," she said, taking his hand and lacing their fingers together as they stood before her easel. "I am not the best at sketching but have made it work. Perhaps you can sketch, and I can turn them into paintings."

He turned her to face him. "I am sorry I called your dream 'nonsense'. I was an idiot."

"I might have muttered something of the like, or even a bit worse, so I'm sorry for that."

"Please don't apologize for being right."

"Theo, I understand your concern about protecting the estates and the title. I wouldn't ask you to go back on a promise to your brother, as long as you don't lose yourself in such a promise." She touched his cheek, and the electricity of her touch reached his entire being.

"Of course you should have your art gallery," he said. "We'll figure it out. As long as we have each other, all will be well."

She snapped her fingers. "I have an idea. Perhaps we keep the ownership of the gallery a secret. The *ton* loves a bit of mystery and intrigue, which would help draw more people to the gallery. We can work through a solicitor to hire the staff to see to the day-to-day management. I can still display my paintings there, and no one will be the wiser."

"I don't know. I don't want you not to take credit for something you have wanted for so long."

She draped her arms over his shoulders, clasping her hands behind his neck. "What I cared about was a place to display my paintings to share with others. And if we can draw in more support with it remaining anonymous, that is more artists we can ensure get their deserved attention. I think it's an even better plan."

"Only one small revision to your plan."

She eyed him curiously. "I'm listening."

"Might my name be included on the pieces we collaborate on? I would like the world to know what an excellent team we are."

She pushed up on her toes, pressing her lips against his for a soft kiss. "I think we can weather the scandal of a marquess who is also a talented artist. Does that mean you still wish to marry me?"

"If you thought for a second I was going to let you toss me aside that easily, you haven't been paying attention, beautiful."

She giggled, and he was addicted to the sound. "I think I should write to Papa and tell him I have fallen in love with the most handsome rake, and that you will call on him at the conclusion of the house party. I don't want to offend our hosts, especially after Eliza and Craven departed only a few days in."

"Can you leave out the part about the rake?" he asked, groaning. "I will have to drag you to Gretna Green if your father should refuse."

She pretended to contemplate his words and then grinned at him. "I suppose you are right. But as long as you know I am not ashamed of who you are."

"Was, sweetheart. That was who I was. And I am forever wholly and completely yours."

"Well, hopefully, you aren't completely reformed because there are certain rakish qualities of yours I find irresistible." She pressed her lush body against his, and he couldn't help but clasp the full cheeks of her arse to pull her harder against him, taking her lips. There would never be anything better than every taste of her.

A knock sounded at the door. "Miss, I came to see if you need anything."

"I'm fine for now, Bess," Juliet called back at the door. "Thank you." She covered her mouth and stifled her laughter.

"We are sure to be caught during the day like this," he said, coming to his dratted senses. "I must depart. Others may notice both of us missing from activities."

She huffed but appeared to agree with this logic. "Meet me in the main salon in a quarter hour. We can join in the activities together."

"I will be there. I'm not certain I have an interest in yard games at present," he said, giving her arse a squeeze. "But at least I'll be by your side and can pummel Duncan if he should look at you in a way I don't care for."

"Be sure to save some of that energy for tonight," she teased. "Assuming you aren't now so full of honor that you won't sneak into my chamber any longer." She released him and started towards the washbasin, smiling at him over her shoulder.

He followed her and pulled her back against his front. It was pure torture having his hard bulge pressed against her bottom, but as always, he was a glutton for punishment. He nibbled at her neck, then soothed the area with his tongue. Theo brushed his lips against her ear. "Leave your door unlocked."

Epilogue

3 MONTHS LATER

Juliet could hardly contain her excitement. She had a present for her husband and only hoped that he would like it. She had carefully draped it with fabric in order to prolong the surprise when she gave it to him. It was positioned in the middle of the art studio that Theo gave her as a wedding gift. It was perfect, with most of the room lined with windows, so she had plenty of light to work from at various points in the day. He had arranged the whole thing as a surprise for her when they returned from their month-long stay in Scotland.

Marriage suited them quite well. She recalled how her father only questioned Theo's intentions for a few moments but could see the love that radiated from him. Her father had given Theo some input on his estates, which he had welcomed and appreciated. The pair had become close, and it warmed Juliet's heart that her husband saw her papa as a fatherly figure.

Eliza had been shocked when Juliet wrote to her about her betrothal to Theo. Nick and Theo knew each other from their university days, so they had quickly become close friends. Theo deserved to have family and friends in his life who cared about him almost as much as she did.

His confidence seemed to grow more by the day regarding estate management, and he even talked as if he was beginning to enjoy it. Not as much as drawing, of course, which he still made time for.

When she wasn't tending to household matters, she was usually in her studio, or being driven to distraction by her handsome husband. His satchel was full of drawings that only the pair of them could ever see, but the memories of him completing each of them would forever be etched on her heart. Especially the memories of the things he did to her afterwards.

She grinned at her thoughts and looked towards the door. She had asked Theo to attend to her as soon as he finished his correspondence. Tapping her foot, she fought her anxious energy. She had been waiting for just the right moment to give the gift to him, and she couldn't wait any longer.

Juliet started towards the door to retrieve him, but he finally came striding in, meeting her right at the doorway.

"There you are," she said, releasing an exasperated sigh.

"Here I am." He reached for her and pulled her against him. He kissed along the globes of her breasts and cupped one with his hand. "Please tell me this is what you summoned me here for," he said, moving close to her neck.

She shook her head, forcing herself not to get distracted by his wicked attention. "No," she replied. "But perhaps afterwards."

He leaned back to look at her. "What is it?"

Clasping his hand, she pulled him with her until they stood before the sheet, which covered the gift she had for him.

"I have something for you."

"Sweetheart, you didn't need to get me anything."

She rolled her eyes. "Will you just remove the sheet and see what it is?"

He eyed her curiously and stepped close to the present. He glanced back at her one last time and then clasped the side of the sheet and carefully removed it, and it fell from his hand as he took in what was on the easel before him.

"Jules," he whispered. "This is…this is…I love it."

She stepped up beside him to look at the painting with him. It was a full body painting of Theo in his finery, looking every bit the aristocratic marquess. She believed she had captured him perfectly, with just a hint of the mischief that always lurked in his eyes.

"I began working on this right after I first showed you the painting of the woman with child."

He smiled as if recalling the memory. "And we were soaked from the rain."

She nodded. "Somehow, I knew then that you were going to be important to me, and I had to paint you. I wanted you to see yourself the way I see you."

"Does this one have to go to the gallery, or can we keep it here?" he asked, but she already knew which he would prefer.

"I painted it for you. It is yours to display wherever you wish. I get to see the real version every day."

He placed a soft kiss on her lips. "I'd like to hang it in my study, right next to the painting of Thomas."

She wiped a tear from the corner of her eyes, understanding what that placement meant to her husband. "Perhaps you should check the name of the piece. I wrote it on the back."

He picked up the painting and turned it around and read it out loud. "Father to our...child."

Theo looked up at her. His eyes shone with nothing but love and joy. "You are? We are?"

She nodded, grinning back at him as a few tears rolled down her cheeks. He set the large canvas down carefully and then pulled her into his arms. "I love you so much, Jules."

"I love you, Theo."

He placed his hand on her stomach. "I don't think there is anything in this world that could make me happier."

"Perhaps if the babe is a boy?" She laughed.

He shook his head. "I don't care. As long as we are a happy, healthy little family, that is all that matters. Speaking of which, when should we tell your father?"

She nudged him towards the settee by a line of windows. "No more talking, unless your words are dirty, husband."

She turned so her back was to him and clasped his hands to pull his arms around her. Once she felt that familiar bulge against her bottom, she rubbed her cheeks harder against his member in the way that always got her what she wanted. It hadn't been difficult to figure out the simple things she had to do to get him in any manner she wanted him.

"Jules," he ground out. She grinned and her core throbbed, anticipating what he would do next.

He urged her to lean over the settee. She rested her knees on the cushions and gripped the back, spreading her legs apart, a position she had been in countless times on the sturdy piece of furniture.

She glanced over her shoulder to see him working his falls. She laughed, noting they hadn't even bothered to close the door.

Theo moved closer behind her and leaned forward to kiss the back of her neck, lifting her skirts to rest high on her back. He inserted two fingers inside of her sheath.

"You have been planning this, my beautiful siren," he said, smirking. "You aren't wearing any underclothes, and you are dripping."

She wiggled her bottom to move against his fingers. "I'm wanton for my husband."

He released a low growl and removed his fingers, replacing them with the head of his cock, then pushing into her with agonizing slowness.

She moaned, loving the way he felt inside her from that position. She rocked back against him, gripping the wood trim of the back of the settee. He clasped her hips and thrust into her.

"Touch yourself," he ground out, thrusting into her again.

She slipped one of her hands between her legs and teased her nub, and he continued his slow, hard thrusts. She circled the sensitive flesh with her fingers and then let her head fall back against him when she came for the first time, clenching hard around his cock and rocking harder against him.

"That's it. Always my good girl," he whispered, kissing and sucking her neck before increasing the speed of his thrusts.

She used both hands to clasp the settee again, supporting herself against the intensity of his fast, hard, delightful movements.

Theo's breath became labored, and she reveled in the power of his thrusts and how feral they had become. Juliet approached the cliff of ecstasy again and cried out when she leapt over the edge, knowing he would always catch her. She moaned and rocked, that climax far more intense than the first. Theo thrust into her one more time before he shifted to short, deep thrusts as he spent inside of her, her name escaping his lips in a soft whisper.

He released her hips and pulled her skirts back down to cover her again. He plopped onto the settee, pulling her to sit across his lap.

"How did I get so lucky for all my days to be like this?" he asked, tucking a loose curl behind her ear. He shifted his hand to rest on her stomach, lightly rubbing her with the tips of his fingers.

Juliet placed a tender kiss on the lips of the man who would forever make her weak in the knees. "The rake surrendered to his muse."

Want more of Theo and Juliet?

They have appearances in the other books in the Unlikely Betrothal series! If you haven't read book one, *The Earl and the Vixen*, get your copy today: https://books2read.com/theearlandthevixen

Here is a look at the full series, and keep reading for a sneak peek at the next book, *The Marquess and the Earl*!

The Unlikely Betrothal Series

A different couple at the same house party finds their match! Who will be next? Each of these books are stand-alone stories complete with a HEA and lots of spice, but recommended reading order is below:

Book 1: The Earl and the Vixen
Book 2: The Rake and the Muse
Book 3: The Marquess and the Earl
Book 4: The Viscount and the Wallflower
Book 5: The Duke and the Widow

Dearest Reader

T hank you for taking the time to read *The Rake and the Muse*! I hope you enjoyed this spicy read, which is the second book in my Unlikely Betrothal series. I enjoyed bringing Theo and Juliet's story to life on the page and can't wait to introduce you to the other couples at the Ockhams' house party!

I am so thankful for all my readers and would appreciate it if you would leave an honest review on sites like Amazon, Goodreads, BookBub, etc.! Also, I'd love to stay in touch, so please visit christinadianebooks.com to join my mailing list and receive a free copy of Only A Rake Will Do (the Ockhams are in that one, too!), and stay informed on upcoming releases, promotions, and current projects.

If you are interested in being on my permanent ARC team and/or Street Team, send me a message on one of my socials! I'd love to chat!

I hope all of you will follow me and get the latest happenings and info on releases from my historical romance friends on any of my socials:

- Website: christinadianebooks.com

- Instagram: @christinadianeauthor

- Facebook: christinadiane

- TikTok: @christinadianeauthor

- YouTube: @ChristinaDianeAuthor

- Twitter: @CDianeAuthor

- GoodReads: ChristinaDiane

- Follow Me on Amazon: Christina Diane

- Follow Me onBookBub: Christina Diane

- Join my Reader Group: The Swoonworthy

Scoundrels Society

Hopefully I left you wanting more, so keep reading for a sneak peek at what is coming in *The Marquess and the Earl*, book three in the Unlikely Betrothal series! I hope you are as excited as I am for Nate and George! You can also go ahead and get your copy of *The Marquess and the Earl* here: https://books2read.com/themarquessandtheearl.

The Marquess and the Earl

NORFOLK, ENGLAND - SEPTEMBER 1814

Nathaniel Baring, Marquess of Demming, watched the fields and trees pass outside of his carriage window. He still wasn't certain that he wished to attend the upcoming house party hosted by Viscount and Viscountess Ockham, but given that he was on the road to join the very event, it seemed the decision was made. His dear friend Juliana, a close friend of Viscountess Ockham, had him included on the guest list, even though she wouldn't be in attendance.

Juliana meant well, hoping that being with others might help him get over his lost love and not hide out in his country estate. Though the man who had captured his heart died over a year ago, he still wasn't certain if he could love anyone else with the same intensity. A carriage accident cost Nate a future that included love, and he'd spent the last year and a half grieving and coming to terms with the realization.

Nate hadn't been intimate with anyone since either, and a house party trapped with men who were vastly different from him would not help him remedy that desire even if he had it. He might not believe that love would come around again, but he didn't believe he wished to seek only his hand to meet his need for the rest of his days.

But it wouldn't be in the cards for the coming fortnight. He would be surrounded by ladies seeking marriage and widows seeking trysts, as well as the gentlemen who would look to partake in whichever of those selections were most appealing to them. It was the way of the world for men like him, living in a society where he could be sentenced to hang if anyone caught him in bed with a man. Yet, even with the risk, it had seemed inconsequential when he had the man he loved at his side.

There had only been one man since whom he thought might be intriguing, but he had misread the man's reaction to him. Fortunately, he figured it out before he made any intentions known towards the man, as that would have been disastrous. One couldn't simply walk into the room and ask the men which of them also en-joyed the other company of other men. Even if he could, it wouldn't mean that he would be attracted to them.

It made the entire business of finding someone that much harder. Which only made him wish he could bring his love back from the grave and continue the life they were building together.

Reducing the numbers to the size of a typical house party would only make his plight next to impossible, so he mentally prepared himself to flirt with a few of the ladies and listen to the men discuss all manner of inappropriate topics over their port. Surely he could survive a fortnight enjoying the same company. He liked the Ockhams when he met them at Juliana's wedding, so leaving with a few more close friendships would be worthwhile.

He sighed, almost convinced that he would enjoy his time at the house party and then retire to his country home again for a long while. Lonely and alone. Juliana was right. He needed to be around people more. Spending so much time on his own would eliminate any chance of love, or even someone to warm his bed, given he doubted that love was possible and a tryst was more probable.

The carriage pulled up into the circle drive of the large, opulent country home of Viscount Ockham. It wasn't as large as his own primary estate, but there was something charming about the light brick manor and beds of roses that lined the entire front of the home.

Once the carriage rolled to a stop, he emerged, not waiting for a footman to open the door for him. He was eager to stretch and move about on solid ground. Brushing the dust from the road off his coat and breeches, he started towards the stairs to greet his hosts.

"Lord Demming, how good of you to join us," Lady Ockham said, appearing at the top of the stairs with her husband by her side. They were a striking couple, and from what he knew of her ladyship, she was a force to be reckoned with.

When he reached the top of the stairs, he took her hand in his and bowed over it. "Thank you for the invitation, my lady."

Lord Ockham extended his hand to him, and Nate gave it a firm shake.

"Any friend of Juliana's is a friend of ours, of course," the lady said. "Perhaps you might even find the one who captures your heart while you are here." Her eyes twinkled at the notion. He wouldn't be surprised if she believed herself a bit of a matchmaker with her guest list, as most hostesses were rife to do.

"One can only hope," he lied. Juliana was the only one who knew of his secret, and she would never tell another soul, aside from her husband, who was surprisingly accepting of their friendship. The couple was a rare breed among the *ton*, for certain.

Lady Ockham looped her arm in Nate's and escorted him towards the entrance. Nate glanced back over his shoulder at her husband, who followed behind them, Lord Ockham's shoulders shaking from biting back his laughter.

"Is he laughing at me?" she asked.

Nate looked between them, unsure who was the most important to keep on his side.

Thankfully, Lord Ockham took it upon himself to respond. "You are just in your element, darling."

She waved him off and continued over the threshold of their home on Nate's arm. "I like you, Lord Demming."

"I like you, too, my lady," Nate replied, almost afraid to say anything otherwise. Although, he found he did like her very much. He also knew she was fiercely protective of her friends, which was admirable in their society.

"Demming, you will find it is best to succumb to whatever my wife has planned for you for the next fortnight," Ockham said, smirking at his wife. "She means well."

Nate was suddenly concerned about what matchmaking attempts she would execute and how he would avoid them.

"Don't worry, my lord," Lady Ockham said as if she read his thoughts. "I won't be forcing anyone on you.

Whom you spend the rest of your life with should be your own choice." She patted his arm. "I was selective in my guest list, seeking the most spirited, intriguing members of society. With maybe a few others sprinkled in to keep everyone on their toes. If love should bloom, all the better."

He smiled at her, relieved that she wouldn't attempt to see him leg shackled by the end of the party. A notion that, in his case, wouldn't be feasible. He wasn't certain he would ever wed, since he wouldn't do so without the woman knowing what she was getting herself into. And it would take an understanding woman to agree to such a match and keep his secrets.

"Baxter," Lady Ockham said, catching the man who appeared to be their butler. "Would you show Lord Demming to his chamber and ensure his trunks and valet are shown there as well?"

"Of course, my lady." The man motioned for Nate to follow him.

"Meet in the downstairs salon after you have refreshed yourself," Lady Ockham said before he departed. "I would like everyone downstairs by six, sharp. Dinner will be served shortly after."

Nate nodded and bowed to his hosts, then followed their butler up the stairs. A smile of satisfaction spread across his face as he entered his chamber, delighted with the room that would be his sanctuary for the next two weeks. He had an enormous four-poster bed, with a set of chairs and a settee before a fireplace. The fire hadn't been started yet, but he was certain his hosts would ensure it would be by the evening, given that they were approaching the season of cool fall evenings.

He dropped himself onto the settee and lay back, reminding himself he would have a pleasant time at the party and worry about the state of his love life, or lack thereof, at a later time.

Nate's trunks had arrived in his room, and his valet, Thompson, helped him to change into suitable dinner attire. Once he was freshly dressed and cologned, he departed his chamber. He was interested to see who from society would make the formidable Lady Ockham's guest list.

He spotted his hosts as soon as he entered the salon where the other guests had begun to gather.

"Good evening."

"Thank you for being prompt," Lady Ockham said, grinning at him. "Do mingle with the other guests. If you require introductions, just let me know."

"I see Onslow over there," Nate replied. "I believe I shall greet him next."

He at least knew most of the gentlemen in attendance from his days at Cambridge, and if not there, he had seen them at various events.

"Onslow, good to see you," Nate said, approaching him at the sideboard.

"You as well, Demming. Was it Ockham or his wife who talked you into attending?"

Nate laughed and poured himself a tumbler of brandy. "Neither. It was a mutual friend of ours, Juliana."

Onslow eyed him curiously, so Nate continued. "She seems to believe I need to get out of the house more, even though she is currently settled at home with her husband."

"These women are quite meddlesome," Onslow said, rolling his eyes.

"So which of our hosts roped you into attending?"

The man scoffed. "The viscountess, of course. She wouldn't take no for an answer. Although, I supposed I could think of worse ways to spend a fortnight."

"Does that mean you are looking at the young ladies in attendance in consideration of being the next Countess of Onslow?"

Onslow scoffed. "Not in the slightest. I'm going to continue enjoying bachelorhood as long as I can. What about you?"

"Same," Nate replied. "I hope to avoid the eager misses seeking the leg shackle."

Onslow held up his glass to him. "I'll toast to that."

Nate held up his glass in return. He knew Onslow from school well enough to know that the man didn't share Nate's interests. Onslow was attracted only to women, but for whatever reason, he fought the inevitable taking of a wife. It wasn't any of Nate's business, since he had no inclination to disclose his own reasons for doing the same.

"I promised our host I would mingle and meet the other guests," Nate said, "and she scares me."

"You had better do as she asked, that's for certain. I am sure we will hide together much of this fortnight."

Nate patted the man on the back and moved about the room with his drink in hand. A pretty blond woman moved out of his way and his breath caught when his gaze landed on the man in his line of sight. He had never seen the man and did not know who he was.

He appeared shorter than him by a couple of inches, which Nate liked. The man was broad-shouldered, with a trim waist. His hair was brown but with golden strands throughout, which were accentuated in the candlelit room. Nate couldn't see the man's eyes since he was glimpsing his profile, but he imagined they must be some kind of blue. At least that was what he hoped.

Nate noticed that the man spoke with a petite redhead. He would consider her quite pretty, with her red hair, adorable freckles, and heart-shaped face, but Nate imagined some of the *haute ton* considered her unfashionable. She smiled up at the man who took Nate's breath away, although her expression wasn't one of attraction. He wasn't certain that she was attached to the man, which was all the better for Nate.

Watching and observing people was something Nate had become very good at. It was a necessity in order to determine if a gentleman might return his interest. So far, he found nothing in the enticing man that might indicate he would return Nate's attraction, and he had every reason to believe the man was courting the redhead. What a lucky chit.

Before Nate could look away, the gentleman glanced in his direction and caught his gaze. He had been right about the eyes, as they were a deep sapphire blue. Something about them made him unable to look away. The man offered him a small grin and gave him a polite nod. He returned the gesture and then forced himself to turn away. He took a sip of his drink, attempting to appear nonchalant, even though his entire body had responded.

Hopefully, the man didn't find him strange after catching Nate watching him. Perhaps the gentleman would think he was curious about the lady in his presence. He wasn't fool enough to hope the man responded to him in the same way. Pining after a man who was only attracted to women was the definition of foolish for someone like him. It would lead nowhere. But it didn't mean he couldn't look and admire the man with no one else being the wiser.

"Are you having a pleasant time?" Lady Ockham asked, appearing next to him again.

"Indeed," he replied, taking another fortifying sip of his drink.

"Have you found anyone you weren't acquainted with?"

He pretended to look about the room before landing on the gentleman with the redhead, unable to stop himself from asking about the man who would haunt his dreams. "That gentleman over there and his lady friend. I haven't met them before."

She looked in the direction he indicated. "Oh, that is the Earl of Knox and Lady Lily Fairfax." She leaned closer as if she were about to tell him a secret. "Her father is hoping he will propose by the end of the house party. Lady Lily is a bit bookish and quiet in public, and her father wants her to wed a peer."

Nate's heart sank further with each of her words. He knew better than to allow himself even a small bit of hope.

"Come with me," Lady Ockham said. "I shall introduce you."

Acknowledgments

There are so many amazing people in my life who have supported me, new and old. Authors and readers! I truly appreciate each and every one of you and hope that you will continue to stick with me on this journey. I would like to call out a few key people, but please know that this isn't an exhaustive list and there are so many people whom I love and adore. I wish that I had room to name them all!

Steve: My husband is the one who continually supports my big and daring dreams, all while providing tech support, cooking dinner, doing the laundry, spitballing ideas with me, and so much more! He's a true partner in every extent of the word and I couldn't do any of it without him. Love you, Babe!

Dexter and Felix: My boys frequently provide me with distractions while I'm in the middle of writing. However, they are also often the inspiration for some of the witty sibling banter that makes it into my drafts. I don't even know what they're going to think when they realize one day that their mother writes smut. Oh well... I love you, boys!

Rachel, Nina & Brittany: I am fortunate to have these ladies (my mom, aunt, and sister) in my life. They have been there for me the entire way and have supported me through the ups and downs throughout the years. They are all used to my crazy ideas and what I can do when I put my mind to something. They just keep cheering me on. They are the ones who hold all of my embarrassing stories and memories, so I can't ever let anyone speak to them without me present. But I love you, all!

Erin: We were destined to be besties from our very first meeting. She is the person I talk to about all the things when I need to bounce around ideas, work on my mindset, take a breath, and so much more! Love you, dearly!

Morgan: None of this could be possible without her keeping the trains moving! If there is something with this biz that needs to get done, she is right there at my side helping move it forward, and she usually comes up with a simpler, better idea! Truly, thank you!!!

Bliss: I can't believe the good fortune we had to have met in a smutty follow train group on Insta, but here we are! It was another fateful moment! I would be sad without our daily texts, talking about our writing progress, smutty scenes, and all the happenings in life. Thank you so much!!!

Courtney: Fate struck again, and I am so thankful to have a partner in crime and twinsie for this author journey! Thanks for all of the ideating, chats, and feedback into the wee hours of the morning! We are going to rock this thing!

Thank you to everyone on my Beta, ARC, and Street Team! (Especially Rachel W., she has literally read every single word that I have written, and I haven't scared her away yet!) The love and care that you put into reading, providing feedback, and helping promote the stories means so much more to me than you know. I hope we get to keep hanging out together for many years to come!

Thank you to Dragonblade Publishing for seeing something in me and my stories! I know I am going to continue to grow in my author career with your guidance and support.

Thank you to all of the amazing author friends and influencers I have met through various social media groups! This amazing community has seriously been one of the best parts of this whole journey, and I am thankful you all let me be a part of it!

About the Author

Christina Diane is a wife and mother who enjoys weaving stories of love and passion from her home in Northern Maine. She is a hybrid indie and traditionally published author with Dragonblade Publishing. Her favorite genre to read and write is historical romance set in the Regency era. She also reads many other genres, especially dark romances and psychological thrillers.

When she is not writing or chasing after her family, she usually has a Kindle in her hand! Along with her husband and two boys, her family includes their three French bulldogs who go everywhere with them, as well as two solid black cats. The entire family is always up for new adventures.

Her writing journey began at the age of nine when she created her own comic strip, Grizzly Grouch. In adulthood, she was a freelance writer for several years, mostly writing lifestyle pieces for blogs. She found that she couldn't stop thinking about stories and characters, so much that she had to get them on the page! Christina frequently has dreams of random character ARCs that go into a massive list of planned writings. She currently has more than ten series just waiting to be written!

Aside from her family, writing, and books, she loves *Bridgerton*, the Grinch, Jessica Rabbit, horror movies, Chucky dolls, cold brew, yoga, *Hamilton*, the color pink, and speaking in obscure quotes from movies and TV shows.

Christina loves chatting with her readers and talking about great reads, so please contact her on socials! She'd love to hear what you think about her books and what you'd love to see more of!

Printed in Great Britain
by Amazon

56615306R00108